DELUSION

A Sonia Amon, MD Medical Thriller

(Book 2)

By

Judith Lucci

Books by Judith Lucci

Alexandra Destephano Novels
Chaos at Crescent City Medical Center
The Imposter
Viral Intent: Terror in New Orleans
Toxic New Year: The Day That Wouldn't End
Evil: Finding St. Germaine
Run for Your Life
Demons Among Us – Coming 2020

Michaela McPherson Novels
The Case of Dr. Dude
The Case of the Dead Dowager
The Case of the Man Overboard
The Case of the Very Dead Lawyer
The Case of the Missing Parts

Artzy Chicks Mysteries
The Most Wonderful Crime of the Year
The Most Awfullest Crime of the Year
The Most Glittery Crime of the Year
The Most Slippery Crime of the Year

Sonia Amon Medical Thrillers
Shatter Proof
Delusion Proof
Fool Proof
Tamper Proof
Obsession Proof

DELUSION PROOF

Bluestone Valley Publishing Harrisonburg, Virginia

Copyright © 2019 by Judith Lucci

ISBN: 9781706790570

Prologue

I'm only aware of fear.

It's so all-consuming that every element of my body is screaming for relief. The muscles want to relax, the heart to slow, my lungs to pull in unsullied air and the blood to return to those paths that keep me alive.

It's my brain that won't relinquish its call to battle and yet can't identify the danger. What is this hell? It's mine and mine alone. It's what makes my days calm and rational by contrast and yet the exhaustion permanently intrudes.

It's behind me. No! It's at my side. No! I risk a backward glance at my pursuer, but he's hidden in the fog. I know it's male; it always has been. It's imperative I escape, not just for myself, but for the others he hunts.

I can do it again, just as I've done it before. I take three long strides with what energy remains and then up! I leap up and take flight. I fight the air beneath my feet as a swimmer attempts to outswim the shark, who she knows is tracking her. Am I high enough? Am I out of reach? Will I be safe?

I need to hide, to blend in with something obscure so I'm not recognized. A bush? In the crevasse of a rock? My body is flexible and if I can just get far enough ahead, around a bend so it cannot track me. I'm desperate for safety.

There! A tree with centuries of age. Its branches bear large, flesh-colored fruits. I push against the air in one last lunge and aim for a thick limb. Success! I wind myself around the limb and brace so I can go forever without movement. My mind goes into hibernation and with that, I am invisible.

The swirl of blackness pauses beneath my tree, and I hear its breath; heaving and moist with the mucus of overly-strained lungs. I cannot pray or else I again become visible, so I watch... and wait.

I hear it draw in a breath of determination, and as I watch, it spins forward, fire and the smell of death in its wake. Soon, it has pursued the wrong path, and I am safe. For now. Until tomorrow... when I must come up with yet another strategy to escape him and survive.

My nausea wakes me, and I'm drenched with perspiration. This wasn't new; in fact, it's very, very familiar and I knew just how long it would be before I re-acclimated to my surroundings and felt safe again. I put my mind through its paces.

The specter that followed could only have been the branches sweeping my window in the rising wind. The black swirls were the fractures of light from the streetlamp at the curb below. The fear was because that's how I've survived. The tree with heavy fruits was my strategy to live just one more day. The scent of death always follows me; it doesn't frighten me. Indeed, it brings with it a sense of failure. Someone I could not get to in time; someone I loved but could not help and perhaps someone whose love I would never have but forever try to rationalize its absence.

I rose from the trampled sheets and heard the familiar floor creaks, guiding me to the bathroom, although I refused to open my eyes. Turning the brushed nickel faucet that I'd so lovingly picked out, I let the water run cold and then scooped handfuls of water over my face.

Sanity returned and with it the relief that the rest of the night was mine to recover. I *would* forget, I swore again. I would forget... and one day I would be free of him.

PART I

Chapter 1

The transport plane touched down on the tarmac in Ramstein, Germany with injured aboard. Although still weak and incapacitated by a broken leg, I hadn't come for treatment, but to tend to Paul. My fiancé was barely hanging on, the target of sniper fire in Aleppo. The only question that remained, beyond that of whether he could survive, was who had ordered him attacked?

As astounding as it might seem, there could be only one answer; one person who would try to kill the man who was closest to my heart. My dead father, Faisal.

That summoned the second, and perhaps the most lethal question of all. Was my father truly dead? Had he managed to outwit American soldiers in a staged leap from a third-story roof, only to have somehow disappeared when they came to inspect his body?

For me, Sonia Amon, the first question held the spirit and security of my heart, but the second held more hatred than I'd thought myself capable of feeling. The Emir, the icon of terror and horror who had continually haunted my life, was still most likely at work. No matter who heard your prayers, it seemed, evil never dies.

Despite my own injuries from being cruelly and sadistically beaten by my father's own men at his order, I struggled to walk off the plane and climb into the vehicle Jeff had waiting for our transport to the nearby Landstuhl Regional Medical Center or LRMC. As we approached the modern façade of the hospital with its curved central structure, fortified by an ultra-modern, unadorned wing, waves of recognition returned. I'd been there before, too many times. LRMC has a wholly unsavory reputation as being one of the largest sources of donor organs in the European region. Mutilated bodies with no hope rolled in one door, and recipients' lives rolled out another. It was a factor of war, not of pride.

It seemed my life was so conflicted. I longed for calm serenity. For a moment my heart cried for Tessa, my beloved dog that I'd once again been forced to board. No matter what had happened, Tessa always provided me calm sensibility with a swift lick of her tongue.

A voice compelled me to pay attention. I was asked for my credentials and handed them over.

"You're retired, Dr. Amon."

"Yes, I am."

"I'm sorry, ma'am, but only military personnel with clearance are permitted past this point."

I looked at Jeff and then back at the young guard with the fresh face and unblemished air of self-importance. I bit back something sarcastic and instead decided to appeal to something more important. "He's my fiancé. I'm also his personal physician, flown in from the States."

The young guard seemed thrown by this; it was a combination of credentials he'd never been presented with before. Jeff sensed his indecision and motioned me with a nod of his head to step back. He pulled the guard aside and told him in a few, very potent and connected words how things were going to be. The guard nodded and motioned me past.

I was unwilling to be in a wheelchair. It was not a place for weakness; but to be brave no matter the cost. I leaned on Jeff's arm but tried to keep it casual if others looked. He escorted me down two halls with railings affixed to the walls. I eyed them with desire but kept going. The further we went, the fewer smiles we saw. The nurses' stations became collections of monitors, and no one was exchanging pictures their children had drawn. These were the halls where soldiers came to live or die; most of them unaware their life was at that point.

Jeff came to a halt before a room with glass walls—various stickers of warning affixed to the door frame. I knew the routine, but it still hits hard when the dangers represented involve someone you love.

Then I saw him. Paul. My Paul. The love of my life. He was surrounded by monitors that beeped, charting his heart rate and aiding his brain in what it currently could not do on its own. Paul couldn't breathe. A huge monster of a machine did that for him. That grieved my heart. His head was swathed in white bandages; his eyes closed and motionless. I knew without talking to his doctors that he had a severe head injury; any head injury is serious. The question lay in what he could do and who he would be if he awakened.

I reached out and touched the back of his hand, careful not to disturb the IV inserted there. Tears pooled in my eyes. Those were *my* hands; they caressed my skin and held me tight when the nightmares came. I could feel the tendons and strength, but now the surface was dry and thin-looking with bruises colored red, purple and blue. It broke my heart. There was absolutely nothing I could do but be there. I couldn't reach him now and that grieved my heart.

"Oh, Paul... I'm here. I hope you can hear me. I'm here for you. It's Sonia, Paul. You'll be fine. You just rest now; you're in good hands." My words choked in my throat. I stifled a cough. He *was* in good hands, as I had always been with him. Once again I yearned for Tessa and a swift lick of her tongue to ground me to reality.

"Jeff, I want to stay." My eyes beseeched him.

Jeff shook his head. "Sonia, you need to rest. The flight, the stress, your leg. Why don't you let

13

me get us someplace to stay, and you rest for a few hours? He'll be here."

I looked up, my dark eyes hungry for encouragement. "You think so? I know you're not a medical professional, but do you really think so?"

He hesitated the briefest second and then said, "I've seen men in far worse shape pull through." A clever answer. Jeff was good at clever answers. After all, he was CIA.

I heard the warning in his voice. I couldn't shake the subtle fear that Jeff had brought me all this way because no one believed Paul would survive. I was, in short, saying my goodbyes. I didn't give speech to the fear. To do so was to change the fates of possibilities. I leaned over and kissed Paul's forehead and then nodded to Jeff, and we ambled back down the hallway and out into the night air.

"Why would anyone do that to another human just because he could?" I voiced my anger and resentment, and both of us knew who we suspected. But there was no proof—at least not yet. I couldn't talk about this with anyone but Jeff. Not my mother; she was the last person. It would be like whiplash to make her relive the torture they administered to her. She still had excruciating headaches from the stoning my father had inflicted on her petite body. At least I was younger, taller, and stronger. My bones had given, but my spirit would not.

DELUSION PROOF

I could have talked to Paul, but for now he was sleeping to hold on to the thread of life within him. I would have to deal with it myself. At least, I would try.

Chapter 2

I left with Jeff and by the time we made it to our rooms, the stress, the journey and the uncertain future for not only Paul but myself, sank in. One can only live on denial and adrenalin for so long.

Jeff left me in my room and went after food while I ran a hot shower and carefully protected my leg as I let the hot water run over my battered body. I looked at myself in the steamy mirror and wondered whether I looked my age or whether the constant fight had taken its toll. With a childhood that ranged from a protected, treasured child to the hunted target of a maniac, there were bound to be some psychological scars. So far, I felt I'd overcome the challenges that had been thrown my way. The instinct for survival was strong; not only for myself but for my patients as a doctor.

Even my career as a physician had been exceptionally stressful. I seldom saw my patients once they healed and regained their lives. I only saw them, lying there beneath my hands with their lives potentially destroyed. I did what I could, and if I was smart, lucky, and carefully observant, I put them back together and sent them off for rehab or long-term care. As soon as I repaired one patient, another potential corpse took his place on the operating table.

DELUSION PROOF

Much of my career, I didn't work in a sleek new hospital with the latest equipment and teams of nurses to assist. Much of the time, it was just the patient and me with death always dangling before our eyes.

Then there was the ever-present threat. My father was hunting for me, and if there was any one thing I knew about him, it was that he believed his reputation and power depended on my being punished for perceived betrayal and that he never forgave.

I sat on the edge of the bed, rubbing my good leg to improve the circulation from sitting for so long. I'd pulled a complimentary terrycloth robe from the hook on the back of the bathroom door and the texture was familiar and very comforting. I pushed both bed pillows against the fixed headboard and leaned back against them.

There was a knock at the door, and it opened. It was Jeff. "Are you decent?" He must have had a duplicate keycard made. Of course, he had. Men in his job left nothing to chance.

"Come in, Jeff," I called across the room. "I'm just sitting here gathering my thoughts."

He closed the door firmly, but quietly, behind himself with his foot. His arms were filled with bags and I saw Styrofoam take-out containers peeking out from the top. "Brought us a little something to eat."

I managed a smile. "Us and what other army? Do you know something I don't?"

"Hey, I have to be good for something, don't I?"

I gazed up at his cheery smile and gorgeous hazel eyes. "Sometimes I can almost stand to be around you," I said, teasing.

"One can only hope," was his saucy comeback as he set the bags down on the table by the window and began unpacking. "Why don't I open the lids, show you what's inside and you pick something."

"Pick yours first," I told him. "I'm so tired. I'm not sure I can eat."

"No, that's fine. I'm the least picky eater you'll ever meet. What sounds tempting? I've got chicken, beef, Chinese stir-fry, naturally potato soup and brats; even some strudel for dessert."

"You're going to spoil me." I smiled at him. Little did he know that I ate Lean Cuisine and Stouffer's almost every night in Washington, DC.

"That's the plan." He winked at me.

One part of my brain heard his thoughtful, endearing language while the other part was screaming that it was all wrong. I shouldn't be sitting here, enjoying a smorgasbord before preparing to climb beneath a pristine white duvet while Paul... well... wasn't. Paul was a prisoner in a cold hospital bed a few miles away hooked up to more machines and tubes than most people could count.

"Just give me the stir-fry. There's a little fridge over there. I can pick at it and finish it as

I'm able." I gestured towards the television set near the mini-fridge.

"As madam requests," he quipped, laying a white napkin over his arm like a waiter. Flipping a fork end over end, he presented it to me with a napkin and the container with the stir fry. I had to admit it smelled delicious. I poked around and recognized chunks of tender chicken, snow peas, soy sauce. The scent of orange marmalade smothering mandarin slices and fried rice hit me. It made my mouth water.

"That smells wonderful."

"I'm glad. Eat your fill and I'll clean up the mess."

"Jeff, why are you doing this?" I stared into his eyes.

"You know why."

There were few secrets between us. Comparable in intellect and experience, we both knew what we avoided discussing. The specter of Paul and the possibility of my father still roaming the earth were concerning topics over which neither of us had control. Jeff was trying to get me healthy again, in preparation for the battles we suspected were coming.

Jeff had been my CIA handler while I was still active. We knew things we couldn't even admit to one another; things we'd witnessed that didn't bear repeating for fear they could happen again. If minds could hold hands, we'd already learned how to do that. Now that I had once again become active, we were again doing the CIA dance.

"Yes, I suppose I do," I sighed and closed the lid. "I'm just too tired to eat."

He immediately set his container down and rounded my bed, folding back the duvet and lifting the sheets so I could slide in my healing leg. "Just lie down for a little bit. I'm going to finish my dinner."

I nodded, and for once, did what he suggested. The bed was luxuriously comfortable, and I only closed my eyes a moment.

There was an odd noise nearby, and I'd learned long before to feign sleep until I could adjust to my situation. It was rhythmic and a little like the monster I'd imagined slept beneath my bed when I was a very young child.

The noise never broke its rhythm, so I ventured to open one eye to a slit. There, next to my bed in a chair, sat Jeff, sound asleep, or so his snoring indicated. His dinner was balanced precariously on his thigh. I'd forgotten how good-looking he was. Appearances were never at the forefront of any of our professional relationships. Survival was.

I wanted to lean over and snatch his dinner container and put it on the floor, so at least it wouldn't land on the carpet upside down. My healing leg was on temporary strike, it seemed, because as I tried to scoot my bottom over to reach him, it shot a deep aching pain from hip to toe.

"Jeff?" I called softly.

His years of standing guard had made him a lifelong light sleeper. He started and just like me, hesitated a few moments before opening his eyes. It struck me how much our lives were affected by what we'd done up to that point. They were things no one voiced and perhaps never even noticed. I wrote it off to my medical training—to be observant of even the slightest change in the norm. It had saved me and others more than once.

I didn't have to say any more. He grabbed the container as it was tipping sideways. "Uh..." he cleared his throat loudly as one does when they're embarrassed. "Wow. Didn't even realize I dozed off," he lied. I knew he'd planned to stay the entire night right at the side of my bed, keeping watch over me as he had so many times before."

"It's okay," I said, smiling as I turned onto my side with my back to him. "Sleep wherever you like; makes no difference to me." I mentally heard his mind working, I swear. Finally, he stood up. "I'm right next door. All you have to do is beat on the wall over your head and I'll be here in five seconds."

"You sure?"

He didn't catch on that I was teasing; a sign of his exhaustion.

"Goodnight, Jeff," I whispered, and he quietly let himself out.

After an hour of heated mental conversations, I finally fell back to sleep.

Chapter 3

Rap! Rap! Rap! Rap! I covered my head with my arms, rolling into a fetal position. *I can't see. It's all blurred. Rap! Rap! Rap!* "Sonia?" *Someone is calling my name! No, not again. Please, not again. The smoke, the blood, the pain..."*

I sat up in bed just as I heard a noise at my door. Someone was turning the handle. Frantically, I looked around for a weapon. Jeff's face appeared then.

"Oh! Jeff! You gave me an awful scare!"

"Really? I've been knocking my knuckles off."

I leaned back, pulling the covers up my chest. "Well, that explains the dream."

"Dream?" he asked as he set down a white paper bag and a cardboard tray holding two of what I hoped were coffees.

"Yes..." I summoned the darkness again, but it wasn't as potent. It would be, though. It came when I least expected it. Jeff was leaning toward me. My reverie disappeared and I took the cup of coffee he held toward me.

"I've got sweet rolls. You know there aren't any better than the German *süßes Brötchen.*"

I drew one slathered with chocolate from the bag and zipped a tissue from the box on the nightstand to put beneath for the crumbs. "You seem to know a good deal about Germany, I can't help but notice."

"I'd venture to say there are plenty of things you don't know about me, Sonia," he answered, his voice slightly mocking. "But, what I came with is good news. I phoned the hospital and Paul is holding his own. He seems to be responding to their treatments to keep him stable."

"Oh, that's wonderful!" I set my cup down and threw back the covers. "I need to get dressed and get over there."

"I only told you that so you'd slow down and take your time. As I said, he's stable and not going anywhere. So, finish your coffee and *brötchen* and then I'll leave you to get dressed. And here," he said, tossing a newspaper onto my lap. "I found one in English. Read it or use it as a tablecloth, I don't care."

"You're thoughtful." I winked at him. He was a good friend.

"All part of the job." He gestured grandly with his right arm. "It's my pleasure."

"Sure, it is." My voice was a snicker.

It felt good to bicker playfully with Jeff; took some of the worry off me. He was right. I needed to heal and that wouldn't happen if I continued to put too much strain on the leg.

"Sonia?"

I looked up at the hazel eyes.

"You mentioned a dream and looked scared when I walked in."

"Well, you barged right in."

"Actually, I knocked more than a half dozen times. You were having nightmares on the flight over, too. I saw them."

"Not exactly a vacation," I said, making my excuses.

"All the same, I want you to see someone while we're here. I'll make the appointment."

"Who?"

"Someone who is trained to help those in transition."

"Oh, I'm fine. I know more about Middle East transition than most people, you know." My voiced sounded surprised.

"Maybe so, but humor me."

I shrugged my shoulders. "Okay, I'll do as you ask. Now run along and let me get showered and dressed. I want to get over to the hospital."

I threw a pillow at him and he caught it handily. "Got your answer?"

"Afraid so," he pouted, but left.

I knew he was attracted to me, but I was more concerned about what waited for me at the hospital.

Paul looked exactly like he had the day before. I hadn't expected any visible change; not unless he awakened. This time I came prepared to stay. By

25

introducing myself to the ICU staff, I showed them respect and they were more open about his condition.

The room was dimmed with the overhead lights turned off. That caused the symphony of lights on the equipment monitors to stand out starkly, underscoring the serious nature of the patient's injuries. The shades were drawn and the equipment huffed, groaned and beeped with regularity. Paul's ICU monitor indicated a normal heart rhythm, a heart rate of 112 beats per minutes and a blood pressure that was surprisingly normal. The gauge that monitored the pressure in his head, better known an intracranial pressure or ICP was in the high normal range. I considered all of this to be good. I checked the settings on his ventilator and was disappointed to find them unchanged. Paul still wasn't breathing at all on his own.

I pulled a chair closer to the side of his bed, slid a second chair to hold my magazines, coffee and purse and settled in for a long haul. Holding his hand, I leaned in close and spoke to him in a calm, consistent dialogue; as though we were at dinner somewhere. I wanted him to get a sense of security and to feel pulled toward me. Of course, my deepest wish was that he'd wake up.

"You know he isn't able to hear you," a harsh voice swept me out of my healing reverie. I turned to look and saw a doctor whose name tag I couldn't make out, obscured behind a coat lapel. He was wearing scrub pants and booties. He'd walked into the room and toward Paul, but then stopped short of the bed.

"Excuse me?"

He looked over his shoulder and then at his watch before answering. "The patient. He's unconscious. Doesn't do any good to talk to him. It makes some people hopeful but a waste. You're probably disturbing his rest." His tone was arrogant and unfriendly. I was appalled.

The doctor angered me, and my heart rate increased. "I didn't catch your name?" I began, standing to get closer.

He avoided my question. "I'm due in surgery. Keep talking if makes you happy." Then he disappeared around the corner and for me to follow meant I'd have to pack up all my belongings, including my charging phone. Plus, with my bad leg, I'd never catch up. I turned back to Paul, quickly going over all the equipment, IVs and the settings on the monitor nearby. The prescriptions matched and nothing was disconnected or improperly dispensed. Puzzled, I resumed my seat just as a black-haired nurse entered with her medication cart. As I watched, she took his pulse, temperature, blood pressure and checked his eyes. None of it was harmful—but it certainly wasn't necessary. Everything she had just checked was already being monitored at the nurse's station. I wanted to ask her about the dark-haired doctor who had sailed past the room, but something made me hold back. There was something wrong. The nurse had unnecessarily duplicated monitored vitals, while the doctor was archaic and wrong in his assumption that Paul couldn't possibly hear me or that I might be disturbing him. Patients sometimes were coaxed from comas by the sound of a loved one's voice.

I had a bad feeling in my stomach. I'd learned the hard way not to trust. Not everyone was who you assumed they were and I wasn't always correct in my assumptions. I decided to be watchful but to keep my counsel to myself for the time being.

Just then another nurse, I knew her to be called Greta when I was there before, walked in. She checked leads and simply gave Paul the reassurance of human touch. "Excuse me," I said softly. "May I see you a moment?" I got up from my chair and walked into the hallway; she followed with a quizzical look. "Could you tell me if there's a duty list available? I thought I recognized a doctor and another nurse and am too embarrassed to ask them to remind me of their names."

The nurse looked confused. "That's not our policy, ma'am. All staff wear their identification tags."

"Oh, I realize that. My name is Dr. Sonia Amon, retired Army. The patient in there is my fiancé."

Greta nodded. "Yes, I've heard your name, Doctor. I will be glad to check with the nurse manager on duty for our department, but the doctors don't report here. I'm new and sorry to say I don't know to whom to refer you, but surely as a doctor, you could ask another doctor in passing? I would very much appreciate you leaving my name out of the conversation; I'm new here and..." she said, letting her voice drift off.

I supposed she was uncertain in her role and didn't want to make any waves. "Of course. Yes, please just ask the nurse manager to stop in when she has a chance?"

"No problem, Dr. Amon." The nurse gave me a confused look and left.

I resumed my seat next to Paul's bed and dug out a small notebook, making notes of the day and time. Reaching out again, I touched the back of his hand and watched his heart rate for any indication that he might be capable of responding. There was no more than a single digit variation; nothing that would be considered significant or hopeful for that matter. I struggled with both the despair someone feels when a loved one is in poor health, and the wisdom and patience of a practiced physician.

My leg ached, and I felt anxious and a little dizzy. I look around the room for some relief. What could be, in emergency situations, a four-patient room had been cleared to just the bed where Paul lay. There was a standard issue wheelchair in one corner and a hospital chair that could recline sat beneath the window. I knew that would be my bed for the night, but for the time being, I wanted it moved next to Paul's bed so I could elevate my leg that had already begun to ache and swell.

"Excuse me, you were asking for the manager?" A stout woman in an old-fashioned white nurse's uniform stood in the doorway, her stance identifying her as a woman of authority. Her gray hair was pushed up into a starched hat and I was put in mind of my old-school secretary, Frances. I was a bit put off. I hadn't seen a nurse in a cap for decades.

"I'm Dr. Sonia..." I began.

"I know who you are." The woman's voice was sharp and punitive. "I'm busy and you're not a practicing doctor, at least not here. Please state your question and let me get on my way." The woman was unfriendly and close to hostile. Now I understood why Greta hadn't wanted to be involved.

She reminded me very much of Frances. They shared the same, no-nonsense behavior. I appreciated that fact because I knew how to appreciate and work well with their efficiency. "Nurse...Daniels," I made out from the clearly-lettered name badge she wore—another relic from a bygone era. "I'd like to speak to a nurse who was in here earlier and I'm told you're the only person who might have that identity."

She puffed up, just as I'd expected. "When was she in here and what did she look like?"

"About an hour ago. She had black hair, braided into a coronet on her head. Olive skin. Dark eyes."

Nurse Daniels shook her head. "No one here like that. You must have it wrong. Not even anyone in the cleaning staff looks like that. That all?" She checked her watch.

I felt the fear her words lit. "There was a doctor who came in the door briefly but left quickly. Broken English, about 38, smallish build?"

"I don't track doctors. You'll have to contact the LRMC Credentials Office, but I doubt they'll talk to you. Can I go now?"

I swallowed my irritation with her dismissive, disrespectful attitude. "Nurse Daniels, you've been most helpful. Thank you for taking time from your work."

She nodded curtly and disappeared. I remembered belatedly that I wanted her help to move the recliner and got up, sliding my leg to follow her. I couldn't have been three seconds behind her, and yet there was no one visible in the long hall. It was empty.

The nurses' station was also empty, which was never supposed to happen. It was an intensive care unit. Patients were to be constantly monitored. *What was going on?* I turned to grab my phone when someone came around the corner. As he came closer, I could see he was carrying a tray. He was young, blue-eyed and had blond hair. His English was slightly accented with German.

"Excuse me?" I called to him.

"Ma'am?"

"Where is everyone? The nurses?"

"Ahhh, there should be someone at the desk, but I guess they were all called in to patients. It is dinner time and some may be on break. May I help you?"

"The head nurse..." I began.

"Betty Schmidt?"

"No, no, Nurse Daniels. Stocky woman, 50-ish."

He shook his head slowly as he thought. "No one here like that, ma'am. Shall I find Mrs. Schmidt for you? You can push the button on the patient's bed, and someone will be right in."

"Yes, yes, I'll do that," I said, backing away, feeling the dizziness and so confused. Paranoia invaded my senses. "Oh, wait! Would you mind pushing a chair for me?" For a moment I saw bright lights and disturbing images, the same image that had plagued me since the Flash Bang I'd encountered in Aleppo. My head was paralyzed with pain and I could barely stand.

He looked around for somewhere to set the tray and balanced it on the corner of the nurses' station counter. He followed me into the room and scooted the recliner over to the side of Paul's bed. I raised my hand in thanks and he left.

I sat in the chair, my head and eyes raging with pain. I sat quiet for a few minutes. When I felt sufficiently recovered, I borrowed an extra blanket from the pile of clean linens next to the clothing closet. It smelled clean and familiar. I held it close to my nose as I pushed the chair flat and took the weight off my leg. Laying my hand over Paul's, I closed my eyes and let sleep take away the confusion and fear. My hand would protect him—I hoped.

Chapter 4

I'm falling. I'm in a tunnel—in a freefall like Alice in Wonderland. Images swirl to form the tunnel walls; some are ablaze and burn me as I pass. Others explode and I'm bounced against the opposite wall. I reach out, trying to find a handhold and just when I think I have one, another explosion pummels me and I lose my grip, spinning again. There is pain... so much pain.

"Sonia!" A voice, very close. It sounds urgent, not angry, but impatient. I feel myself being slowed as if some giant hand is gripping my shoulders and the pain and heat recede.

Then, I'm free. The air is cool and clear; I can breathe. The dizziness has left and while I feel somewhat trapped, I'm able to move. I open my eyes and they're drawn to the monitors, flashing green eyes and jagged smiles that never leave the screen. I hear that familiar, almost comforting sound as they beep. This sound means everything is stable. It's that faster, louder sound that signals alarm. But it is that explosive sound that I dread the most, for it likely means someone will die. Or, the explosive, fast sounds and then no sound at all.

"Sonia?"

I look toward the voice and Jeff comes into focus. I try to sit up, but my legs are wrapped in the blanket.

"I could hear you. You were having a nightmare. I didn't want to shake you too much and yet I could see you were having a bad time."

"Oh, Jeff. I'm so glad you woke me. It was horrible. I was falling and everything hurt. I couldn't come out of it and I heard your voice." My attention flew back to the bed. "Paul."

"I think he's pretty much the same. There have been nurses and doctors in and out, but they just check the monitors and touch him on the face. They don't tell me anything."

"Jeff! Here, wait, let me sit up." I operated the lever on the side of the recliner and the sudden upright movement made my head swirl for a moment and I saw flashes of light. *Damn that flash bang...* "Listen. I know this may sound alarmist, but there's something very strange going on."

"Such as?" Jeff raised his eyebrows.

"Earlier, there was a doctor who came by as I was talking softly to Paul. He wasn't America nor German. Accent and irregular English, most likely Middle-Eastern, at least originally."

"What about him?" Jeff had known me long enough and, in enough crises, to recognize my concern. He gazed at me steadily.

"I think he was coming in to tend to Paul and heard me speaking to him. Told me it was useless and suggested that I disturbed him. That's not true. I asked him for more information, but he left quickly. Disappeared. Later, there was a nurse in here who took vital signs which is unnecessary since Paul is already connected to those monitors. After that, I asked to speak to the head nurse, who came in and was short and brusque. I described the vital signs nurse to her. She blew me off and said there was no such nurse like that, and she left. I stepped out to call her back to help move this chair, and she'd disappeared. The nurses' station was empty. Jeff, that's *never* supposed to happen. Finally, an orderly came down the hall with a meal. I asked him about the head nurse I'd met and he said there was no one here by that description. I laid down after that and then you woke me."

"Is your leg hurting you?" Paul looked at me but ignored my story.

"Some, but that's to be expected, particularly when thrashing around in a chair. But the rest, Jeff. Something very strange is going on around here. People are coming in to tend to Paul who I don't think are supposed to be here. I'm concerned, and you know I'm not an alarmist." I held his eyes with mine.

Jeff nodded. "True, but I also know you've been through the mill and just made a major trip to get here. That *must* have some effect on the body. Plus, you're probably still jet-lagged. If you were suspicious of one person, I'd be concerned. But three? That sounds more like you dreamed it."

"But," I protested. I was mad because he was blowing me off.

"No, no," he held out his hand, "I get it. Let me get you some food and give you time to orient yourself. I'll bring you a tray from the cafeteria. Then we'll talk."

I nodded, suddenly feeling like I was the patient and Paul was an unconscious victim, as well as my responsibility. Truthfully, maybe that wasn't so far from the truth. It wasn't like Jeff to disregard what I said and it hurt my feelings, not to even mention my ego.

I got to my feet. Using the chair to steady myself until I regained my equilibrium, I stepped into the tiny bath. Tidying myself, I splashed cold water over my face and the back of my neck. The woman in the mirror looked tired and not all that well. I knew I was pushing my boundaries by coming, but Paul was my fiancé and needed my help. I loved him. There was a comb in the nearby patient personal care kit. I used it to make some sense of my hair and could hear my beautiful mother's voice in my mind. She would tell me that looking your best was good medicine. In many ways, she was the wisest person I knew, and in others, she had the vulnerability of a young child. Perhaps I'd gotten the best of both my parents and yet that warred within me. My father hated me and wanted me dead. He'd already tried to kill my mother and me both. *That* was not good medicine.

I was just coming out when Jeff walked in, a large tray with covered dishes piled high. "Got a few things. Most of them will keep," he commented as he set them on the rolling over-the-bed tray pushed to the side of the room.

"I guess you *did*. Were they having a sale?" I tried to smile at him, but my anger was still fresh.

"One thing I'm here to tell you is that I'm leaving. Headed for Syria and Grayson's command. I wanted to get you a bit stocked up on food. Now you can make fewer trips downstairs."

I smiled. "I think they'll bring meals up, Jeff, but you're sweet to think ahead for me." Smiling, I laid my hand on the back of his and he didn't budge. I could sense strength in his flesh and bone hand. It felt every bit as supportive and strong as the one he'd extended to me when I got into trouble in the past, acting on the CIA's behalf. He'd been not only my handler, but my friend. I compared his living hand to Paul's bruised hand and swollen fingers. Jeff was here and he was alive. I didn't know where Paul was.

He cleared his throat and I heard the emotion he was trying to swallow. He slid a metal chair, the seat upholstered in green vinyl, closer to me and sat down. "Look at me, Sonia."

I sat in the recliner, reaching for a Styrofoam cup with ice water. I nodded and leaned toward him. "Of course, Jeff, I always do." My heart raced. There was something in his voice that concerned me.

He shook his head. "I hate to say this, but... Now, *you* know and I know who may be behind this." He was referring to Faisal Muhammad, my father and the most powerful terrorist the U.S. had encountered. He was the man who wanted to end my life—there was no forgetting that, either. "Officially, the Agency is operating under the assumption that he was killed jumping from that roof. You and I have talked about the possibility that it was a set-up and he's been lying low, waiting for the right opportunity to surface and kill."

I nodded and could feel my throat tightening and a rush of cold descending down from my head to my gut. My stomach cramped with anxiety.

"Unofficially, they're giving me an opportunity to join Paul's command and see if I can find more concrete proof, one way or another. As much as I want to stay with you, and Paul, of course, I think I can be of better service at this point to do what I do best. Collect and process information. That's the best weapon the U.S. can ever have against your father, or his replacement—however it turns out. So, I'm leaving tonight. In the meantime, you stay here with Paul and in a few days, they'll airlift you both back to the States, to Walter Reed."

I nodded. I didn't want to see him go, but everything he said was sensible and in my emotional state, I needed to let go of control and just be there for Paul.

"Now, there is no way I would leave you to fend for yourself, as well as oversee Paul. I have someone here who is one of us. Ester, would you come in, please?"

I looked over my shoulder and my mouth dropped open as the young nurse with the dark-haired coronet and sultry eyes who I'd seen earlier walked into the room. "Jeff, this the nurse…"

He was nodding. "I know, I know. Sonia, you're the smartest woman I know and normally I would be all over this report of the unusual hospital personnel. I can prove to you that Ester, at least, is safe and here to look after you. She checked on you before I came, but I'd asked her not to divulge who she was until I had the chance to talk to you. She'll travel back to the States with you, but in the meantime, she blends well and speaks several languages. If there's something concrete going on, she will immediately report it to me and we'll evacuate you both. I'd like to avoid that because it exposes us and tips our hand."

I nodded, content just to listen to a competent, strong man take charge. I was so tired of all the running, the suspicions and the pain. "Thank you, Jeff. Ester, it's nice to formally meet you. But what about the others, Jeff? The head nurse and the doctor? Who were they?" My voice was rushed and anxious. I noticed how Ester gawked at me.

"I can't answer that, and maybe never will. But Ester is very competent, and she will be your eyes and ears. You know how to reach me if you need me, but as I said, my efforts are better spent getting to the bottom of our suspicions. After that's been determined, I'll join you back in the States." He grinned at me. "Not so bad, is it?"

"I hate to see you go." I was feeling sentimental and very, very lonely.

His hand covered mine this time. "It's the best way for me to keep you safe."

I nodded. "I know."

"There's one other thing I want you to do for me."

"Anything."

"I want you to see someone, one of us. He's highly-trained in PTSD." Jeff locked eyes with me. I felt deceived and angry.

"I don't need that." I tried to control my anger, but I was furious. I felt as though Jeff had betrayed me.

"Let's let him be the judge of that. His name is Dr. Milliken, and he's the best."

Milliken. Ugh. I detested Milliken. I looked down at the floor, signifying the end of my interest in the conversation. I had to be reasonable, though. Jeff was doing his best. "Not him again. I don't like him, Jeff. Always asking me how things make me feel. Not very helpful and I don't need him to tell me that none of this makes me feel safe or happy, or even strong enough to keep going. He'll want to put me in the hospital for observation." I stared at Paul. I was as resistant as I'd ever been. My stomach churned at the thought of seeing Dr. Fish Eyes, my nickname for Dr. Milliken.

"And you don't want that?"

I gave him a withering look that was answer enough.

"Okay, I get it. But it's the best I can do for now. I want someone monitoring you—even if you don't like his manner. Do you think every patient you've treated always loved you?"

"Not fair."

"Okay, I'm reaching here, but the point is, my job is to find the root threat and your job is to manage the symptoms. Deal?"

"Deal."

"Good." He stood up and bent to kiss the top of my head. I wondered if Ester hadn't been watching whether I might have tipped my chin upward to catch his kiss on my lips. "Promise me you'll be cautious and don't push yourself. However it turns out for Paul, remember you have me," he said before leaving the room. His words echoed in my head, leaving me with a good, safe feeling. Jeff had always been that for me. A safety net in the middle of hell.

I patted the empty chair. "So, Ester, sit and let's come to know one another."

She slid onto the chair, careful to face the door while not being rude to me. She was well-trained for threats; that much I could readily see. But, the look on her face suggested she didn't want to sit.

"You are educated as a nurse?" I began the conversation.

"Yes, ma'am. I'm an RN." Her voice was short, her tone staccato.

"And your nationality? Where are you from?"

Ester's eyes looked straight ahead. "My parents are Turkish but emigrated to the U.S. a decade before I was born."

I recognized her accent was convincingly American, tinged with perhaps a bit of somewhere else. "Are you from New York?"

"Yes, ma'am." A smile blossomed on her face. "I'm surprised you can tell."

I nodded. "Well, let's just say I've done my share of travelling. So, tell me, Ester. Are you with the Agency?"

Her look was immediately guarded. She countered by saying, "I'm trained and qualified to look after you and Colonel Grayson. I speak six languages, including German and Farsi and hold a post-graduate degree from George Washington University in nursing and another in law."

"Ah, I see. One of the Foggy-Bottom students." She blinked slowly, refusing to acknowledge. I could tell she had very little sense of humor, if any. She'd be the quiet but competent companion. Ah well...I'd hoped she'd be more entertaining. We had a good deal of rough water ahead of us and keeping the atmosphere light was always a healing strategy. But at least she knew what she was doing and of the two, that was by far preferred. I left it at that and went silent.

I opened one of the covered dishes Jeff had brought, renewing a pang of regret that he'd left. Why was I suddenly feeling so sad and abandoned? I'd always been strong, confident and ready to take on any assignment. I was going soft and I hated that thought.

A chicken breast and green beans with a side of mashed potatoes and a chunk of cornbread stared back at me. Good old American food. I loved it and was sure that the patients considered it a treat after rations in the field, even if it meant that being here was due to having been injured. "Have you eaten, Ester?" I offered her the plate.

"Yes, ma'am. I'm all set. That food is for you. I'm provided for."

"Very well. I can tell you're not much for chit-chat so I'll let that hope go. Instead, I'd like you to go over the records for the Colonel's treatment plan and please compare any medications to what are hung there for his IV. No one is allowed into this room without my approval and they are to present valid credentials before administering medication or conducting any type of treatment. If it becomes necessary that the Colonel be taken to another part of the building, let's say for some sort of testing, either you or I must accompany and remain with him, at least visually. Is that understood?"

"Dr. Amon, I don't mean to be impertinent but with all due respect, my assignment is to protect you and the Colonel. I've been briefed on procedure in this case and have my orders. In short, I not only understand, these requirements have been anticipated and no matter what you request me to do, I cannot do it if it conflicts with my orders, ma'am."

Her posture was tall and strong. God help me but I couldn't take any more uber strong women! Even though I was one myself, I was at a time in my life and my needs that I wanted to be simply Sonia. Female, and perhaps even boring, might be nice for a change. The alternative was Dr. Milliken and those horrid, dead fish eyes of his.

I nodded and said nothing more but continued to watch. After all, two sets of eyes were better than one. To her credit, Ester carried out exactly what I'd requested without further comments, so I must have fit in with the plan.

Thank God.

Chapter 5

Paul was no better, but he *was* stable. I don't believe his doctors at Ramstein would have considered transporting him if it weren't for the fact that I would be accompanying him, along with the mysterious, terse Ester.

I found a way back to the utilitarian hotel and left Paul in Ester's hands. I badly needed a solid night's sleep or I would need my own doctor on the flight home. I showered and then eased my leg onto the bed, situating pillows for support. I don't think it took longer than five seconds for me to fall soundly asleep, and that night, gratefully, my dreams were silent. I awakened feeling better than I had in some time and ordered up breakfast before I left for the hospital. There I found a sleepy, but vigilant Ester.

"I'll take over while you get some sleep," I told her.

"Ma'am. The doctors believe that the Colonel is stable enough for special transport, so I've taken the liberty of making the arrangements. We will be departing at 1600 hours. I will get some rest and rejoin you here at 1400 hours to prepare for the transfer. Here is my phone number and I'm only a block away. Don't hesitate to call if you need me."

"Thank you, Ester. That's quite efficient." I was pleased at her efforts.

"Ma'am," she acknowledged and then I was alone.

Thankfully, Ester had left the recliner next to Paul's bed. After checking him personally, I settled stiffly into it, the familiar noises of an ICU establishing a rhythm in my brain. I held his hand and then read to him from a military news website. I'd decided to keep life as normal for him as possible. It was incentive to wake up and to fight. Once a soldier, always a soldier. They rose to the challenge and that was how I hoped to get Paul to respond.

My phone buzzed for my attention. "Hello?"

"It's Jeff, Sonia. Just checking in to see how things are going and if there's any news."

My heart warmed to the sound of his voice. "Paul is stable, and the doctors are releasing him for transport today. Your Ester is a marvel at organization. She relieved me overnight, so I got a good night's sleep and she is resting now. She has arranged transport. We're leaving at 1600 hours."

"Good. Yes, I cleared the transport. You're all set, and it should be good weather, so you'll have a smooth flight. Let her shoulder the responsibilities, Sonia. She's up to it; you know I wouldn't bring in somebody you'd have to supervise. You just focus on yourself... and Paul, of course," he added as an afterthought. His comment caused me to think.

"Anything there?" I knew he wasn't free to talk, but we had our own little way of communicating we'd developed when I was actively working on behalf of the CIA and he'd been my handler. I figured our call was on a non-secure line.

"Not yet. Just getting things sorted and then I have some leads that need walking." His voice was matter-of-fact.

Even though I was disappointed there was no news, I was happy to have his friendship. "Take care and be safe. I don't know what I'd do without you." I intended the remark to be casual and what you'd wish for a good friend, but inside I felt it more deeply rooted—almost a part of my psyche.

"How are *you?*" Jeff sounded concerned. "Are you up to the trip"

"Yes, of course I'm up to it. I'll be fine. No further incidents." I wasn't sure my voice convinced Jeff.

"I'll be in touch. Take care, Sonia." The line went silent.

I knew Jeff had to make a special effort to call; it wasn't encouraged, especially when neither of us was stateside. I appreciated the effort and it made my afternoon warmer.

True to her word, Ester walked in the door at 1400 hours carrying a small bag from which she extracted a notebook. She began taking note of

Paul's set-up and reviewed the medical plans with the doctor and nurses. We were going to the airfield by military ambulance and then by air transport to the States.

I did as Jeff asked and left things up to her. She was quietly efficient. In a way she reminded me of my younger self; a time when the medicine and mission occupied all my attention. It had been my way of coping with my childhood. People had no idea what a dysfunctional family was all about until they reviewed mine.

I'd let my mother know I would be overseas for a short period and naturally she gave me every objection she could think of. Despite my own capability, she liked to believe, as all mothers do, that her presence could keep me safe. In return, I never let on that I thought my father could still be alive and a threat; I would become aware of his presence in time to protect her—at least I hoped so. That was one of the reasons I was in Germany and Jeff in Syria. My second reason was simply to look after Paul.

There was roughly an hour before we were due to leave. I elevated my leg now as I knew there would be some walking and a good deal of sitting involved during the transport. Ester came back from planning. "When are we leaving for Syria?" I asked her.

She turned and looked at me straight on. "Ma'am?"

What part didn't she understand? "When are we leaving for Syria?" My voice was clear. I wondered what she didn't understand.

She cocked her head and said, "Ma'am, I believe you mean the U.S.?"

"No, of course not. Syria. That's where Jeff is waiting for me. We're going to Syria." My voice was insistent, and I felt my blood pressure rise.

"Ma'am, you're traveling with the Colonel and me back to the States via aeromedical evacuation, ultimately to Walter Reed. You're not going to Syria, ma'am."

But Jeff is waiting for me. He needs me to help find my father, if he's still alive. I said no more but nodded. Jeff had told me to trust Ester and let her take the reins, so that's what I did.

I didn't notice that Ester had left the room. I still wondered what was wrong with her.

Chapter 6

Although I'd been aboard them countless times as a physician, I continued to be impressed by the efficient and yet full-service aeromedical planes. With an open cargo bay of a full 88 feet in length and 18 feet in width, capable of cruising over the Atlantic at 515 miles per hour, they were more than impressive. Even that power still required a double crew at every assignment as these impressive air transports generally flew return missions as soon as new patients were loaded, exceeding the time limitations a solo crew member could be on duty. As it was, our transport had already made the eight-hour trip from Syria to Ramstein where they'd changed crew and been refueled. The second part of the journey would be heading over the Atlantic to transport Paul and another handful of wounded soldiers back to the U.S. Factors such as altitude, temperature control, lighting, stability and oxygen aboard a flight ambulance were major considerations and personnel, even those who were already medically trained, underwent special courses prior to administering to patients aboard. I had completed my training and would be on hand for duty only if necessary.

The flight was long; longer than I'd remembered, but then I hadn't been under the

51

stress this trip required. Once Paul was loaded and properly connected to his tubes, paraphernalia and machines, I watched the physician examine him. When I was satisfied things were in order, I took my seat nearby and buckled in. It felt good to be going home. I would need to let Jeff know that I wasn't coming to Syria. I still wondered why Ester was so confused about that.

We touched down in the States and by all appearances, which were later confirmed at Walter Reed, Paul had endured the trip quite well. His vital signs were stable and he seemed to be at relatively the same place he'd been when we left Ramstein. There was no change whatsoever. I was disappointed. I guess I'd expected him to sit up and talk once we hit American soil. It was just a dream, I guess.

Exhausted, I left him in capable hands and headed toward my house outside D.C. When I retired, I'd given up the more ostentatious apartment and bought myself a small brownstone. I poured myself into a shower and then into bed. I took the risk and texted Jeff briefly:

Home. Patient safe. Won't be joining you, sorry.

Then I gathered the pillows around me for support, flipped on the television to catch up on any news I might have missed and fell asleep before I turned it off.

DELUSION PROOF

I awakened early, while there was still peace in the morning. I lay there, staring at the ceiling, watching the morning light creep across its expanse and thinking. My life has never been placid, nor has it been easy. Simply giving yourself peace to think is a luxury I'd recommend.

I needed more time to think, to recall and sort out the intricacies that affected my life. I was healing, inside and out. My father had done a number on me a few months ago and I was still reeling from the pain and memory. Paul needed me. I needed Paul. Even though I knew he'd be in the best hands possible, I wanted to be personally involved in every decision and aspect of his care. At the same time, my healing was making me feel slightly diminished—even confused. I was aware of it and knew it would be temporary. The confusion was still frightening. I knew it was one reason why I didn't want to see Dr. Fish Eyes. There were too many people and events depending on me for me to be confused and I knew it. I vowed to get more rest and recover.

My thoughts wandered to Jeff, in Syria at that very moment. I hoped he could ignite an otherwise cold trail that would prove, once and for all, whether my father was dead or alive. Hoping my father was dead went against everything I believed in, everything in the natural order of things. It was certainly against my instincts as a healer. But still, I wished him dead and I decided not to do battle with that and just accept how I felt.

I worked hard to absolve myself of guilt for my feelings on this. I told myself he had placed himself in that role the first time he killed; the first time he tortured, and especially when he abused, tortured and attempted to kill my mother and me both. As a child, his kidnapping hadn't seemed so unnatural—after all, he was my father. It felt like my mother had left. As his parenting skills became malicious and I grew old enough to understand the truth of what had happened, I began to replace love with hatred. The most effective way for me to think of him now was as a cruel and vindictive killer, and not as my father. *My* father died long ago, just after I was born. The man who later assumed that title had, in a sense, killed my father and *that* was the man I now hoped was dead. If he wasn't, my mother was in as grievous danger as I was. Then there were the other innocents, those he would order killed in the name of his own supremacy.

I doubted he was dead. A small piece of my soul and a piece of my inner mind just knew it. He was too smart to let himself be captured. It would be very predictable for him to engineer a way for him to fake his death but affect an escape. In fact, that described almost everything about him— duplicitous. He delighted in drawing you in with what you dreamed of having and then pulling it away at the last moment and substituting it with sickness and evil that never ended. His perversity was potent enough to create a lifelong dread in my mind as to whether he was searching me and my mother out to destroy us. I felt like an ant in a sandwiched ant farm, going about my business unaware that my demise was being planned. It was the worst cruelty imaginable.

My thoughts jumped to my mother. Melody, my well-meaning, sweet-natured mother who'd had no clue as to what she'd led us into. She could not have predicted the peaceful man of Islam could become an international terrorist. She couldn't have predicted Faisal's maniacal tendencies and the perfect storm of terrorism cells, weapons and an endless supply of funds to back them. When my mother met him, by all accounts he was a peaceful man, a man who loved his beautiful American bride.

A cold feeling washed over me and I could feel my heart pounding. The ceiling, once placid, non-threatening plaster, now swirled dangerously and I had to close my eyes against the dizziness. Pulling the covers to my chin, I waited for it to end. The fear, the uncertainty, the pain of seeing others die and knowing that my mere existence may be contributing—it was all getting to be too much. Perhaps, in one sense, I was responsible for Paul's critical situation. I was sure *I was the reason* he was shot.

One never knows where the ripple effect will originate, but I, for one, felt guilty.

Chapter 7

I finally arrived at Walter Reed much later than anticipated. Frances, who always seemed to anticipate what I did before it occurred to me to do it, was waiting with coffee and a cheese Danish. "You didn't bother to eat, did you?" she chided me. I shook my head, used to her hovering ways. Frances shook her head as though I was hopeless. Perhaps I was. I was however, cheered when she rolled her eyes and grinned at me.

I was currently only able to practice as a physician consultant. After my injury, and most particularly the flash bang, I'd apparently made a few medical "judgement errors" and had to be certified fit to practice again. I'm not sure the "errors" weren't part of a medical turf war with a colleague, but regardless, I couldn't engage in solo practice. As a doctor whose work was the primary focus of her life, this felt almost claustrophobic to me. It was my essence to heal and to be denied the opportunity felt punitive. It was yet another reason to hate Faisal Muhammad.

"How's the leg?" Frances wasn't being polite; it was more like she was documenting intel. The Army was her life and I had to respect how she felt given that I felt similarly in my desire to be on duty.

"Healing." My reply was clipped.

"Are you keeping it elevated?"

"Who is the doc here, Frances?" She was my secretary, but took liberty with that responsibility.

She was unperturbed. "Your mother phoned. She'd like you to call her back."

My mother. My sweet, patient, loving mother who was now ignorant of Jeff and my suspicions. I wondered whether I was truly doing her any favors.

I nodded. "Thank you. What's on my agenda today?"

"You have an appointment in twenty minutes with Dr. Milliken."

"Reschedule it." A lump formed in my throat. I couldn't abide that man!

"No can do. You have to face him eventually, Dr. Amon. May as well get it over with. You're smarter than he is. Piece of cake." Frances shrugged her shoulders and dismissed my objections.

"I appreciate your encouragement but the whole thing is completely unnecessary." Frances went by the rules and although she refused to call me by my first name, she evidently had no scruples when it came to bossing me around.

"Doesn't matter if you think so. It comes from the Command, and you know it. Now eat and drink up; you need to be there in fifteen and by the look of your limp, you're already late. Would you like me to call for…"?

"No wheelchairs, Frances," I interrupted. "Leave me a little dignity, will you?" I scowled at her.

"Yes, ma'am. Tick tock."

I rolled my eyes at her busy-body impertinence. Somehow, she made the cold, sterile environment of the hospital feel more like home. I couldn't do it without her.

Dr. Sydney Milliken, or as I knew him, Fish Eyes, held court in a small office at the end of a corridor where those with mental impairments were kept. Merely walking down the hallway gave me a sense of unease. One negative word from him and I could be prevented from practicing medicine forever. For a moment I wondered what it was like to hold someone's future in your hand. It was exceedingly difficult to be honest with him when so much lay at stake, and yet I suspected he wasn't easily fooled, no matter how tricky I thought I may be. I'd decided my tactic would be to say no more than strictly required.

"Good morning, Dr. Amon. It's good to have you back."

Why did he care where I was? "Thank you, Dr. Milliken. Good to be back." *I had to force myself not to stare at his unwholesome appearance. I doubted he was married. Who wanted to sleep next to a dead fish at night? I figured he was probably cold and slippery too.*

"Why don't you have a seat? May I get you something to drink." The cold fish eyes looked straight through me.

"Thank you, no." I could be curt, too; professional training.

"How was your trip."

"Uneventful."

"Could you elaborate on that, please?"

I even hated the sound of his voice. No doubt the fact that the man held my future in his slimy hands accounted for most of my dislike.

"I'm sorry. The transfer went as planned. No surprises. Colonel Grayson is resting and in good hands."

"I'm glad, but we're here to talk about you."

I sighed. *Here it comes.* "What would you like to know about me?"

"Have you had any more episodes linked to the flash bang?"

"Such as?" I shifted my leg to be more comfortable and I saw his eyes go to them. Was he a lecher or did he read something into the fact that I shifted position when asked an undesirable question? Both, in my opinion, were equally unwelcomed.

"Visual or auditory sensitivity, either the lack of or overly compensatory?"

"Nothing I've noticed." My cast was itching, but I'd be damned if I was going to move it a centimeter.

"I see." He paused. "So, have you heard anything or seen anything that no one else saw."

"What?" My voice was sharp. "What are you talking about?" I stared at him.

Fish Eyes turned a few pages in my chart. "It was reported that after the Flash Bang you had some visual hallucinations and just a few weeks ago, you thought someone was talking to you who really wasn't." His cold eyes stared me down. He dared me to contradict him.

"No." I shook my head. "I've had no visual or auditory hallucinations. I can assure you I'm not psychotic." I hope my voice wasn't as angry as it sounded. I was dizzy with anger for a moment.

Dr. Milliken nodded slowly. He made some notes on his iPad. I ignored him and thought of myself as an ant that was moving one grain of sand forward at a time. Soon, I'd have my escape tunnel dug and then Dr. Fish Eyes would be in my past.

"Let's move to another area. Dr. Amon, have you noticed any periods of confusion, anxiety, depression, anger or other emotional reaction?"

There it was. He was going for the subtle things that couldn't be proven, or disproven, for that matter. These were the quick sands of psychiatry; those amorphic diagnoses that would allow him to prescribe and I would be obliged to consume whatever he prescribed whether I wanted to or not. My life as a physician, my practice, was in his hands.

"Nothing remarkable." I treated him like I was reading an x-ray.

"Uh, huh... are you acquainted with a nurse named Captain Haran? I believe she accompanied you on your flight back?"

"Captain Haran? Oh, you must mean Ester. She never gave me her full name and title. Of course. That was just yesterday." I hadn't meant to add that last. I saw his tactic; to provoke me into revealing more than I was willing.

"Yes, indeed it was. Dr. Amon, she reports that you had a period during which you insisted you were to travel to Syria, to join... ah..." He flipped a couple of screens. "Jeff Hansen. Do you recall this?"

Sweet Jesus, had I done that? Or, did Ester make that up? If she made it up, why would she? I had no idea what she might have gained by fabricating my behavior, but I'd learned over the course of my lifetime that no one could be trusted. Not even a parent. Especially a parent in my case.

"I'm not aware of it, but it's possible I had a slip of the tongue. After all, I was dealing with jet lag, leg pain and the stress of my fiancé's condition."

"I see." He stared at me and I wanted to poke a stick at him to see if he would flinch. "Is there a reason you would be going to Syria, Dr. Amon?

According to your records, you've retired from such assignments."

"I *am* retired. Most likely a sleepy slip of the tongue." Obviously, Dr. Fish Eyes didn't know about my "other" assignments – assignments that would take me back and forth to the Middle East for years to come.

"And yet Captain Haran reports she had just relieved you for a full night's sleep." He looked up to catch my facial response and I tried to make my eyes as plastic as his.

I sighed. This had become a game of cat and mouse. I was clearly the mouse. "Dr. Milliken, I believe the short turn-around of the trip, the jet lag, the fact that I was feeling anxiety over the health of my fiancé and was in a hospital where I had no ability to care for him personally added up to the sufficient logic of an unintentional slip of the tongue without seeming unduly extraordinary."

I knew as soon as I'd said it that once again, he'd baited me into a protracted explanation. That was a sign of anger. *Damn!*

"Dr. Amon, are you feeling particularly stressed in this meeting?" His cold eyes searched my soul.

I had to be truthful. "I believe, given the same circumstances and power you hold over my career, you would be equally as uncomfortable."

He was now on a roll. "Do you believe this examination is unnecessary?"

"Yes, I do."

"Why?"

"I believe your field of practice is vital for some, but not for me. While I'm not certified in psychiatry, I have had extensive training and experience in the field myself."

"I see. So, let me ask you a question, Dr. Amon. If I were to be wounded, let's say, shot; would I be better served to try to remove the shrapnel and repair the damage myself, or to see, let's say, someone such as yourself?"

"Does that question require an answer?" I flinched. He had me on that one.

"I see you grasp my point. Regardless of what you think of me or my specialty, I believe you suffer from PTSD and that treatment is indicated."

I said nothing. I couldn't trust myself to speak. As long as Dr. Milliken believed I suffered from an *untreated* emotional or mental impairment, I would be unable to practice medicine. He knew his diagnosis before he even greeted me. Ester's report certainly had put the last nail in the coffin.

"What do you think about that diagnosis, Dr. Amon."

I got to my feet. "I believe, Dr. Milliken, that everyone gains perspective based on their experiences, although *some* of us laid our lives on the line to survive. Who better to recognize what our patients need and be able to provide that?" With that, I left his office and for all I knew, quite possibly, my career. It was a foolish thing for me to do. I knew that, but it was something I *had* to do.

"Well, that went well, Dr. Amon," Frances commented when I returned to my office.

"How do you know?"

"It's all over your face. He should be glad you weren't armed with a scalpel."

"Frances, is it so obvious? Do I appear impaired at some level?" I was frankly shocked by Frances' observations.

"No, ma'am. If my diagnosis counts, I would say you've just gone through some rough water but you're strong and a resilient soldier who can separate her personal and professional judgements."

"Thank you, Frances. Now, would you mind going down and telling Milliken that?"

"If you think that would help."

"I'm kidding, Frances. No, I've done what I was ordered to do and now it's up to him and the advisory board to determine my fate. For now, I'm going upstairs and visit Paul."

"Yes, ma'am. And don't forget to call your mother."

"I won't."

Standing in the elevator, I leaned on the handrail that edged it. I was tired. No doubt about it—healing takes a lot out of you in ways you wouldn't imagine. I had a newfound respect for the patients I'd treated and then chastised because they didn't appear to be doing their physical therapy or returning to duty as soon as expected.

The doors opened and I wanted to sit a few minutes. I spotted the family waiting room and saw it was deserted. That made it ideal and I'd call my mother at the same time.

"Mom?"

"Sonia. I've been waiting to hear from you. Don't go so long between calls, dear. You know how I worry."

"Yes, I'm sorry. I flew to Ramstein. Paul was shot by a sniper in Syria."

"Oh, my god, I'm so sorry. Is he okay? I mean..." She didn't want to ask the inevitable question and I didn't want to answer it.

"We're at Reed now. They're looking after him. He hasn't regained consciousness yet, but he is stable. I was just on my way to see him when I stopped to call you."

"Oh, then don't let me keep you." Her voice was soft but I could tell she was upset.

That was my mother. The happy-go-lucky girl with butterflies and sunshine in her hair had become a worried, stressed shell of her former self. It was a reminder that it's possible for a man to kill a woman without ever touching her, although he'd done that, too. He and his minions had pelted her soft, sweet countenance with rocks. Some of her bone bruises still hadn't healed.

"I'll be by in the next day or two to see you, okay?"

"Yes, yes. Stay with Paul. He needs you more." Her voice was rushed.

I couldn't hang up—not yet. "Mom?"

"Yes, darling?"

"Be careful, okay?"

I knew as soon as I'd said it, I shouldn't have. All the years we'd hidden from my father, we'd uttered that phrase to one another with a unique meaning. We could only be prepared. We'd never be strong enough to vanquish.

"Sonia?" Her voice was sharp. It accused me.

Just as I'd thought. She recognized the secret tonality. "Just don't fall or anything, okay?" I laughed, trying to play it off. "One of us in a cast is enough," I joked, and she giggled, evidently choosing to buy it. She was smarter than that, but it didn't bear talking about.

I disconnected and opened the door to the broadcast. "Code Blue. Code Blue. Room 636."

I stumbled and my heart stopped. My hand reached for the hallway handrail. *Don't let it, don't let it.*

Chapter 8

I dragged my bad leg and used the handrail to vault myself down the hallway, even to the point of pushing my way around a man in a wheelchair. It was Paul's room and the flashing red light over his door confirmed my worst fears. Unable to treat him myself, I had to content myself with standing outside and watching through the glass wall, out of the way of equipment, the crash cart, as a dozen physicians, nurses and staff responded to him. I watched as syringes flew in the air and bloodied gauze was dropped to the floor. I heard them say **CLEAR** three times. I saw the paddles strike his chest. I saw no movement on his monitor. Tears dropped onto my cheeks; tears of frustration, tears of anger. Tears that begged for him to wake up as I bargained for a higher being to bring back the love of my life. Most of all there were tears of hatred for my father, the Emir. Ever since I was a child, I cried when I was powerless.

Dr. Evans, a long-time friend and one of the best in his field stood at the foot of the bed and barked orders like a general deploying his troops. The room was in havoc; chairs and trays pushed aside or even overturned as every square inch around the patient was utilized.

I continued to watch. They did not give up. I knew the routine so well... so well. I knew how often the patients made it and perhaps that's where the new flush of tears began. Syringes were being pushed, chest compressions were ongoing, and the paddles were being charged. His head had been lowered flat and the man whose body had wrapped itself warmly around my own on cold nights lay unresponsive, as though he was part of the bed itself.

I should be in there. I should be adding my skills to those already there. I knew it wouldn't happen, even if I'd been cleared to resume practicing. I was too close, not objective. I would have been asked to stand away.

The orchestra of equipment and personnel knew their parts and played them well. I didn't spot one minute error or hesitation. I watched the monitors and saw the flicker at the same moment they did. They had a heartbeat!

Compressions stopped as all faces were turned to the same monitor. Postures began to relax, people moved away from the bed. Equipment was pushed to the side of the room and Dr. Evans moved to Paul's side. He examined him, particularly looking for any response from the brain. He turned and issued a last set of orders and then emerged from the room.

"We've stabilized him, Sonia."

"Bert, what happened? I thought he was stable?" I'm sure I looked like a crazed maniac.

Bert shook his head. "Have to wait for the labs. He was fine until that moment and the monitors went crazy. Then he coded. We had no reason to think he'd go bad. C'mon, let's have a cup of coffee in the lounge."

He drew me by the arm, allowing me to lean against him. I was still wobbly from the close call. He pushed open the door to the physicians' lounge and we went in. I collapsed on the sofa, overcome with a sudden anxiety and yet exhaustion. "I don't understand," I whined, sounding like the loved ones of so many others I'd treated and had no answers to give them.

Dr. Evans shook his head for the second time. "You're not alone. We'll run some more tests and see if we can figure out what happened and we'll do some neurological testing as well to see if there's been any change in the brain activity. That was close, Sonia, as you probably saw. Very suspicious."

"Suspicious?"

"You and I both know that at that level of external support, there are generally only two options. Either the patient awakens or the brain activity completely flatlines. His wounds are healing, and the body trauma is disappearing. He is, other than in terms of consciousness and brain activity, healthy, extraordinarily healthy."

"Well, I'm not so sure his heart is healthy since he just arrested."

Bert nodded. "We'll follow that, Sonia."

"What are you planning, Bert?" I felt angry and my voice challenged him.

Dr. Evans shrugged his shoulders. "Like I said, we'll wait for the lab and tests to come back and regroup. If necessary, I'll replace every piece of equipment in the room and ask for a guard 24/7." He shook his head, thinking out loud. "At first I thought it was exactly that—equipment failure. But it wasn't."

I sipped the black coffee, even though I hated it without cream. It was almost as good as downing a stiff whiskey. I didn't know what to say, so I remained silent as his words sifted through my mind.

"Are you sure about that? That it wasn't an equipment failure?" Tears burned behind my eye sockets. My throat felt dry and parched from the bitter coffee. "Do you think his code was caused by someone here – did someone sneak something in his IV?" My voice ended on a hysterical note. "Someone has already tried to kill him. We know he's a target." I stared at my long-term friend.

Bert put his hand on my shoulder to offer me comfort. It only felt heavy and my shoulder sagged. "Now, Sonia, my orders for you are to go home. You've not recovered enough to hold up to all this. The trip to Germany, healing, the stress of Paul's injuries... too much in too short of a time."

I shook my head. "I want to stay. I need to watch him." I paused. "For God's sake, Bert, I need to *protect* him."

"We've got that covered." Bert and I locked eyes.

"No, you don't understand." I opened my mouth to object.

He paused. "Understand? Understand what?"

I bit my lip. I wanted to tell him about the strange doctor and nurse no one knew in Ramstein. I wanted to tell him we suspect the Emir was still alive and constructing his personal attack. I wanted him to know that Paul was still in danger—my father had men everywhere. But I couldn't. If I did, I could kiss my license good-bye. For good. Bert Evans would be obligated to report it to Dr. Fish Eyes.

"It's just about having a loved one who is sick, and you feel like you could help," I finished up, hopefully closing the conversation.

He nodded and patted my arm. "Go home and get some rest. If there's any change, you'll be called immediately."

I watched him leave and dumped the rest of the bitter coffee down the sink. With a sigh, I pushed open the door and started down the hallway, pausing a few minutes to look at Paul through the glass. I turned to leave and noticed the man in the wheelchair. He was the one I'd almost tipped over. I headed for him. As soon as he saw me coming, he masterfully maneuvered the chair

180 degrees and powered himself away from me. "Excuse me! Excuse me," I called after him. "I just wanted to apologize."

He stopped momentarily. I caught up to him. "I just wanted to apologize if I knocked you a-kilter an hour or so ago. You see, my fiancé is in the ICU and had an incident."

He nodded but didn't say anything. I walked around to face him and held out my hand in apology. He looked odd in the surroundings as he was well over seventy, shriveled with an olive complexion of someone who had spent a lot of time in the sun. The wrinkles around his eyes were from squinting in bright light. His dark brown eyes were shrunken into his sockets and he had a jagged scar on one temple. He nodded and briefly took my hand before powering himself backward and then around me to continue down the hallway.

Maybe I am nuts, I thought. I'm certainly not looking at the world in the same way. I stopped by my office, picked up Tessa, my beloved dog from my office and headed out. I'd had enough.

Chapter 9

"Sonia, come in, sweetheart and sit down. I was just having some coffee." My mother smiled at me as she leaned down and scratched Tessa's ears.

"That sounds good."

I followed her into the kitchen, reaching for a coffee cup from the shelf because I was considerably taller than her. "Have you ever asked yourself how you could have given birth to a daughter who is so much taller?" I looked at her diminutive stature, partially bent from the pain of beatings.

"Perhaps you are the child of the postman?" she quipped. Her blue eyes shined with humor.

"If only that were true," I said and then we both stopped, amazed at our words. We hadn't talked about *him* since his *death*. We were on dangerous ground. For one thing, if he was alive, he would have spies and even Melody's house might be bugged, as well as my own. We would have to be very careful not to discuss him. The casual comment could trigger his anger and he would release his demons on us. How could I let her know this without making her live in fear again?

She set out a small plate with some home-baked oatmeal cookies and handed me the cream. There was nothing like coming home to heal the ills of both body and spirit. I watched as Melody grabbed a bone for my dog. Tessa loved my mother and often stayed with her when I traveled. Her tail wagged in anticipation of a treat.

"How's Paul?" My mother's voice was concerned. Her eyes searched my face.

I raised my brows in a doubtful expression. "Just as I hung up with you, he coded. They brought him back, but I don't understand why he coded. He shouldn't have. There was no physiological reason for it to happen that we know of. He's practically run on machines at this point and unless one of them fails, we could keep him on life support for decades."

"What happened then?"

I shrugged my shoulders and reached for a cookie. "I don't know. Dr. Evans was on duty and supervised the resuscitation. He doesn't understand why he coded either. He seemed a little suspicious and will be getting the results of lab work and the scans. If something or someone is interfering, they'll get to the bottom of it."

Melody's mouth flopped open. "Interfering? Who would interfere? Paul's a decorated hero." She paused. "Can you help him?"

I pursed my lips. I may as well tell her. "Not yet. I'm suspended pending continued evaluation of my injuries. Mom, I must tell you. There's a chance I might not be able to practice any longer." My eyes filled with tears. "I... I could always teach, do research or go on a lecture circuit, corporate medical professional, that sort of thing." I rolled my eyes. That was certainly not something I wanted to do.

"Why on earth? I don't understand." My mother's eyes were dark with disbelief. "What actually happened?"

"When that Flash Bang detonated, it could have caused some long-term damage, depending on how close I was and whether the percussion damaged soft tissues in my ears and head." I looked at the floor. "It did. I have issues with lights and sometimes I hear things. Apparently, I've made a few errors."

Melody reached for my hand and took it in hers. "Sonia, I am so sorry. You must be devastated."

I blinked back tears. "Then they're trying to say I have PTSD, post-traumatic stress disorder. That means that I could suddenly see something that isn't there, have nightmares, get depressed, confused, anxious—it's treatable but likely to stay with me."

"From Syria?"

I nodded. "From the beginning, when I was a child. It all adds up."

"And do you have any of these symptoms now?"

"That's the million-dollar question. I think I'm just recovering from my recent trauma, but this psychiatrist - who isn't my favorite person - wants to make a bigger deal of it. He has the final recommendation to the medical board on whether I should be allowed to practice."

"Oh, Sonia, that would be just awful. After you've worked so hard." My mother's eyes were sad.

"It's more about the experience I've had treating men in the field and knowing how to recognize the most common weapon injuries. It could mean life or death to some of them."

She reached out to pat my arm. "Honey, what is meant to be will be. Maybe, if you have this post-whatever... maybe it's a good idea to change what you do. Not be working every day with war. It hardens a person."

I considered that. It made sense. "Maybe you're right. Hard to say. I just know that if I can't do what I've been doing, I want to be the one who cuts the ties. I don't want them to get rid of me."

"How do they "see" these things if they're in your head? I don't understand."

I took a deep breath. "There was a nurse assigned to us while we transported Paul. She told the shrink that I made some reference about needing to go to Syria. I think she made it up, but..."

"Sonia? Why do you need to go to Syria?" Her words were slow, measured and suspicious. She was too smart to overlook something like that.

"I don't."

"Sonia...? You tell me the truth now." My mother flashed me 'the look' she'd always given me as a child when she wasn't sure I was telling the truth.

"Mom, I'm retired. I gave that all up." I hoped she believed my little white lie.

"What are you not telling me?"

"Nothing." I patted her arm this time. "Don't worry so much," I urged her. "It's not good to worry."

She leaned forward and hugged me. "My sweet daughter. If we did not worry, what would we have to talk about?"

I really didn't have a response to that and gave her a peck on the cheek good-bye.

I checked in with Walter Reed on arriving at the house. It had been a long and frightening day. I was ready for a hot shower, comfy clothes and a good dinner. Before I undressed, I checked the refrigerator for dinner makings and realized I'd have to go to the store first.

I picked up my insulated bag and walked out the door to head to the grocery. I just wanted to grab a steak, a bottle of good wine and the makings for a salad. I was in and out in under ten minutes.

As I returned from the store, Tessa and I came up my walk, I could have sworn I saw the curtain move in my living room window, right next to the door. I froze, waiting to see if it moved again. I realized I hadn't locked the door when I left; it was a bad habit of mine I'd developed after the Emir had been killed. It was my way of daring him to come after me again. This time, however, the old alarms began to ring, and my arms sprouted chill bumps. Tessa growled deeply. *Something wasn't right.* My heartbeat escalated.

I turned, grabbed Tessa's leash and hurried back to my car, starting the motor and driving down to the end of the block. I sat in the darkness and watched my house, but nothing and no one appeared. I called 9-1-1 and asked for an officer to come.

The squad car showed up roughly ten minutes later.

"Hi, listen, I'm sorry to bother you but I ran out to the store and foolishly left my front door unlocked. When I was going back in, I thought I saw a curtain move. Could you just do a quick look-see? I live alone and with the leg, well, you can see I couldn't run away, and I wouldn't be much good at self-defense." I gave the officer an apologetic smile.

He smiled. "You're Dr. Amon, aren't you?"

"Why, yes, I am. Did we meet?" I was at a loss and a little confused.

"You saved my brother's life when he came back from Iraq. I'd be honored to help you out." The officer smiled at me. "He still sings your praises."

"Why, thank you." I was pleased.

He looked over his shoulder and motioned to me. "You stay put while I check it out." I nodded as he spoke into the mic that was fastened to his shirt shoulder and then went toward the house.

The officer pulled out a large Mag flashlight and pointed it at the windows and under the bushes at the front of the house. He turned and gave me a thumbs up and then headed around the house toward the back door.

I sighed, relieved that my night wasn't going to be scary after all when a tremendous noise hit me, causing me to curl up with my hands over my ears. The sound deafened me. I stayed that way a couple of seconds and then sat up. Terror spun my brain as realization set in. My house was on fire! It had exploded! Tessa barked incessantly even though I hugged her close.

I called 9-1-1 as I quickly started toward the house and then stopped, knowing that someone was watching. This was no accident. I already heard sirens from responding vehicles and knew there was nothing I could add. I got back into my car and waited. Firetrucks and ancillary equipment pulled up, and men were running with hoses toward the fire hydrant. Others began to evacuate the houses nearby. A slow fire was one thing—an explosion was something else entirely. I was heartsick about the young police officer. I'd saved his brother but managed to get him killed, murdered actually. It's funny how irony works.

My way was blocked to get closer with the car. I watched as neighbors poured out, got into cars and were let out between the barricades. I drove up to one of the barricades and told the firefighter who I was and that it had been my home that exploded. He spoke into his shoulder mic, and I was asked to leave the vehicle and go with him. I nodded, opened the door, and when he saw my cast, he told me to hold up. "There was a police officer there," I cried. "I thought I saw someone in my house and called to have an officer check it out. Then came the explosion!" Tessa! Tessa licked at my hand. Thank God I hadn't left her alone in the house.

"Yes, ma'am. We've found the officer. Please stay where you are, and we'll have someone bring up a wheelchair. You'll need to go down to the precinct and answer some questions."

I began to panic, my heart racing, as that cold, unfamiliar feeling began to pour through me. I wanted help; a familiar face who knew all about me and would be my advocate. There was no one. No one I could call. Jeff was still in Syria. My mother couldn't be dragged into this and even Frances, although she knew me well, didn't have all the details of our suspicions. I began to cry and somehow that eased up some of the tension. I'd have to let people know eventually; after all, I had nowhere to live.

An hour later, I was seated at the police precinct, wrapped in a woolen blanket against the probability of shock. Tessa was at my side. I'd given the officers my driver's identification. I knew the car had been searched because they insisted I take a breathalyzer. I guess they thought I'd drunkenly blown up my own house.

The police officer who had answered my call had died instantly in the explosion. That made my heart ache. I had caused a death. I was a doctor and had often been on hand in field hospitals when soldiers died. Death was never witnessed casually; it never grew old, or at least not for me. The idea that this officer had died due to my request for help was especially painful.

There was no doubt in my mind what had happened. I even had to feign being surprised when the detective came in and said the fire department suspected arson. There appeared to be a tripwire that ignited my natural gas. Luckily, the explosion hadn't gone beyond my house. The neighbors were once again safely home. That confirmed my suspicions. The Emir's people were experts in explosives. They left the houses around mine intact not out of kindness, but so that I would know, without a doubt, if I survived, that I'd been the target.

The detective had endless questions. I asked him for some coffee, and while he was out of the room, I used my cell to call a number I hadn't called for a very long time. Jeff was out of the country, but there was always someone at the Agency number. I stalled, and sure enough, within a half-hour two men in dark suits appeared at the precinct and escorted me out. I don't know what the detective thought, but the Agency would make it clear that he should not investigate any further. They had it. They had me.

Chapter 10

Slouching against the cushions of the back seat, I didn't ask questions. Tessa sat beside me and licked my hand. She knew I was stressed. No one spoke to me. That was how the Agency worked. They had orders, and no matter what you said, their orders came first. Therefore, it was useless to argue.

Streets became familiar, even through my sleep-deprived eyes, and when we finally pulled into a parking garage, I recognized the building.

We were at Jeff's apartment.

I was ushered upstairs where I found two women putting away food in the cabinets and refrigerator. A third was putting fresh linens on Jeff's bed, the only one in the apartment. He led a life of solitary secrets. In short, he belonged to the Agency and neither cultivated nor demanded a wife and family. It was just too complicated.

One of the agents came up to me where I sat on the sofa, introducing herself only as Agent Smith. That was fine—names really didn't matter. "Ma'am, per orders you are strongly requested to stay here until an alternate arrangement can be made. I will be the first of three agents assigned to watch the door and all you need do is call out, and whoever is on duty in the hall will come in. You're to enjoy the comforts of this apartment and make yourself at home. Are you in need of any medications?"

"No, no, I'm fine. I don't have any clothes or toiletries, though."

"You'll find that's already been taken care of and in the bedroom," Agent Smith finished. "We'll leave you now. Please make yourself comfortable, and we ask that you not use your phone."

I nodded. I was too weary to argue if there was even an argument to be made.

"Agent Smith?"

"Ma'am?" She turned toward me.

"Colonel Paul Grayson... he is in the ICU at Walter Reed..."

"Security has already been posted, Dr. Amon, per orders."

I nodded. "Good. Thank you."

She left, and I heard her try the door handle to make sure it was securely closed. It was all I could do to make my way into the bedroom, turn on the shower, and then crawl into a pair of military issue pajamas that were laid out on the bed. I hadn't eaten all day, so I headed for the fridge and was overjoyed to see meals already prepared and in containers ready to be microwaved. I had to hand it to the Agency. They knew how to tuck someone away. A few minutes later, I was sitting on Jeff's bed, munching my favorite stir-fry and watching the television news to see their take on my exploded house and the officer who lost his life. Tessa lay beside me. They'd even known what brand of dog food she ate. Amazing! But a little scary, too.

Selfishly, I felt sorry for myself and the number of people who had died near to me, simply because of who I was. It wasn't supposed to be that way. I was a healer, sworn to take care of people.

I panicked as I realized I'd forgotten someone. Shuffling to the door, I knocked. "Agent Smith?"

I heard her close to the door. "Do you need something, ma'am?"

"My mother."

"Already taken care of, ma'am. Have a good night."

I don't know how long I slept, and there was an odd chemical taste in my mouth when I awakened. I suspected someone had been ordered to put a sleeping pill in my food.

I wasn't sure who had door duty. I knocked. "Hello?"

There was a click, and the handle turned. A woman in an obscure dark gray suit came in. "I'm Agent Smith," she said, and I gave her a puzzled look. She smiled at least. "Makes it simpler for you to remember our names and doesn't matter to us."

"I see," I nodded. "I want to know about my mother and Colonel Grayson."

"Both are status quo, ma'am. Your mother has been taken to a secure location pending orders.

The Colonel's condition is unchanged. They knew you'd want to know as soon as you were awake."

I touched my tongue. "That reminds me. Did you...?"

"Yes, ma'am. Orders. They felt you needed more rest."

"Thank them, whoever they are, would you?"

"Yes, ma'am." Maybe I imagined it, but I thought I saw a ghost of a smile flicker across Agent Smith's face.

I turned toward the fridge to make some breakfast and looked over my shoulder to offer her some, but she'd slipped out the door again. The coffee tasted wonderful, and I flipped on the news. The story of my house had disappeared from the line-up, and I felt badly for the police officer who'd died at my house. I'd led him into a trap that was meant for me. If only I'd realized that in advance. In my stupidity, I assumed if anyone came after me, it would mean kidnapping and torture. I was afraid someone had been sent to grab me, but never to blow me up.

Dressing in ill-fitting Army issue pants and a starched shirt, I did my best to curl up on the sofa. I turned on a channel that promised a line-up of mindless game shows and soap operas. I couldn't bring myself to watch the news or any drama, especially anything military. I just couldn't go there for now.

At some point, I must have drifted off because I was awakened with a hand on my shoulder. Tessa lay on the floor next to my bed.

"Sonia?" came a deep voice. I opened my eyes, and there stood a very bedraggled, unshaven and slightly sunburned Jeff.

"Oh, Jeff!" I pulled his head down toward me and wrapped my arms around his neck, nestling my cheek on his chest.

His arms came around me. "It's okay, honey. I'm here. You're fine, and so is your mother. Why don't you let me wash the stink off and then we'll talk? That coffee looks pretty good."

"Oh, yes, I'll have some waiting," I called at his retreating back.

Jeff was quick, and I was surprised when I saw him in sweatpants and a striped robe. He'd never been that casually dressed around me before. He was always dressed as Agency people dress or wore an Army uniform. He still looked tired, but I knew from experience that he was used to going without sleep, sometimes for days. I handed him the coffee. He sipped it, nodded, and pointed for me to sit down on the sofa. Walking to the door, he opened it and requested the current Agent Smith to relocate to the end of the hallway. He closed the door, turning to me to say, "We don't need this discussion to go further than this room."

I nodded and waited.

"Now then. How are you? I mean, *really,* how are you?" Jeff stared at me and tried to read my mind.

"My leg is aching, but that's to be expected. I'm jumpy, but there again, that's to be expected. I'm worried about my mother and Paul and most of all, I'm scared to hear what I know you're about to tell me."

He sipped his coffee again and then set the mug on the coffee table, ramming his hands down into the deep pockets of the terry robe he wore. "Sorry about the clothes, by the way," he smiled, nodding at my stiff and uncomfortable outfit. "We'll get you fixed up with something more appropriate later today. For now, you need to listen to me, but stay calm."

I nodded again. I trusted Jeff with my life. In fact, I'd done so many times.

"Let me start at the top. Your mother is fine. She's only been told that we believe you've been targeted, perhaps by someone in your father's organization or by a disgruntled jihad soldier who has since come into power. She's staying at a nice place, a spa, in West Virginia. The Greenbriar, if you know it."

I knew it. It was a beautiful place, high in the mountains of the George Washington and Jefferson National Forest, and rather inaccessible, except by air. Far beneath the colonial-fashioned hotel was a former command center built during the Cold War. It was said a president could run an entire war from that bunker. "Thank you, Jeff." I was grateful. Even though my mother was the daughter of an impressive political family, Jeff always went over and above his duty for her.

There was more. I looked into Jeff's eyes. Whatever he had to tell me wasn't good. I could feel it. "Well, what else?"

Jeff looked past me, outside at the blue sky. "It's not good and it's about Paul."

My stomach plummeted and I felt nausea rise into my throat. For a moment the blinding lights reappeared in my brain and I was confused. Jeff watched me carefully. "What?"

"There has been another incident, I'm afraid, but he's been stabilized again," he hurriedly added as he saw my eyes widen in alarm. "The Agency has stepped in to analyze records and data to determine whether these are flukes that are manifested physiologically or are a bona fide attack against the Colonel. Right now, we're taking the stance that these are flukes. It closed too many old debts to think your father was dead. I don't know of a single individual, except you and I, who thinks he survived or has any interest in opening that can of worms. So, the Agency is taking the "out of sight, out of mind" stance. That's not to say we can't prove them wrong, and that's one of the reasons I'm back. I think we can."

Our eyes locked. "So you're sure Faisal is alive?"

Paul nodded. "I think so. Yes." He offered me a half smile. "Sorry."

"Thank you. I was feeling vulnerable and for good reason. I have some things to share as well."

"Okay. Hold those thoughts. Here's the deal. "From now on, going forward, you and I are operating under the premise that the Emir is alive and well, and busily planning an attack. We believe it's primarily on you and Melody although any collateral damage will suit his purposes as well."

I interrupted. "Do you know where he is?"

Jeff shook his head. "No, but that's not as critical as you might think. Their technology has improved, and he can conduct his campaign of terror from anywhere in the world."

I rolled my eyes. "Terrific. Even from here?"

Jeff nodded. "I'm afraid so."

"How can I help?"

"Right now, the best thing you can do is stay here, out of circulation. It's decently secure and you'll always have at least one guard, myself included."

"But this could go on for months, even years, Jeff."

"We'll deal with that when we come to it."

"What happened with Paul? What did they do to him?" My heart didn't want to know, but my brain did.

"Like I said, he's stable again, although the doctors feel there's been an overall decline due to the stress of these, incidents, as we'll call them. He has been placed under military watch for the time being."

Anger spread throughout my body. "How could anyone get to him in a military hospital?"

"Actually, Sonia, you can answer that better than I. How many people come through that building daily? What sort of security could protect one patient from intended harm and yet allow entry to families to visit their loved ones? Do you recognize every staff member who comes and goes from his room? It's not a perfect situation, you know."

"No, I suppose nothing is perfect, but his caregivers could be limited. He could be assigned the same staff each shift. That could be controlled. Can we make that happen?"

~~Jeff~~ nodded. "Of course. I'll work on it."

I nodded. "So, what do I do in the meantime? Stay here and play with my dog all day?" My tone was sarcastic but I didn't care. After all, someone had just tried to blow me up and that was a huge problem.

"As I said, stay here with me. I will come and go as normal, and no one will suspect a thing. You were brought in during the night. The building itself belongs to the Agency, although you would never know that. Everything is monitored."

"But where can I sleep? You only have one room?"

"I'll bunk on the couch. Tessa can sleep in the room with you."

"Oh, no, I couldn't put you out." I was dismayed at taking this hard-working man's bed at night. He had to be exhausted.

"This isn't up for debate. You take the bedroom. I'm fine out here. I've slept through many a Redskins game right on those very cushions where you sit."

I agreed, although only under orders. "I'll need some clothes."

"Since the building is secure, you can use my laptop to order whatever you need online. They'll accept UPS packages downstairs – but use my account, so they come in my name. Agent Smith will bring up whatever you order. In the meantime, feel free to explore my wardrobe or wear what you're wearing. You should be able to get something delivered by tomorrow."

I shook my head. "I've got meetings, Jeff. Bills to pay, people to contact. I have a life. How can I do that and stay in hiding?"

"That will have to do for the time being. You can pay bills if you use my laptop and my account. We don't want any activity showing up on yours. You can pay me back when this is over if you insist."

"So, just sit here?" The idea appalled me. I'd never been one for idle moments.

Jeff laughed. "I know, to the famous Dr. Amon, sitting here is like being placed in solitary confinement. Who knows? You might come to like *Dr. Phil,* or binge-watch *The Game of Thrones.* In between, you can cook. Do you know how long it's been since I've had decent meals? Order the ingredients here from the local grocery. They deliver."

"You've got this all figured out, don't you?"

Jeff laughed again; a pleasant sound of confidence in my troubled, confusing world. "I guess you could say it's my job."

"So, what did you find out? What do you know about Paul?" If my voice sounded anxious, it's because I was anxious. I was not sure I wanted to hear Jeff's response.

A flicker of anger crossed Jeff's face. "Okay, now down to that. Paul was shot by one of Faisal's snipers just outside Aleppo. He used a Russian weapon and the sniper escaped. Paul's lucky to be here, I might add."

"Did they shoot him because of me?" Once again guilt paraded up my back. I focused on the floor and scratched Tessa's ears.

Jeff shrugged his shoulders. "Listen, Sonia. Faisal is an unstable man. He's an unpredictable nutcase, and that's what makes him dangerous. You know that!"

I shrugged my shoulders. There was no need to respond to stuff I already knew.

Jeff continued, "The only thing we know about him that's consistent is his hatred for your mother and now you. The fact that you both escaped is a black mark on his reputation."

I smiled to myself. I hadn't thought of that. I rather liked the idea that his fellow terrorists were talking behind his back. I nodded.

"He wants you dead, and I don't think it's simply personal. I think he just wants to accomplish what he says he will do. It's how these people maintain their respect and power base - by terrorizing not only their enemies but those close to them. Hitler was the same way. No one is safe. That keeps down the challenges and the sub-plotters who want to take them out. All that does not make you responsible for anything. Not for Paul being shot or the attempts on his life or your life or even Melody's life for that matter."

I nodded. "I suppose I understand, but I'm not certain. Too much is being thrown at me at one time and my thoughts are getting jumbled.

Maybe Dr. Fish Eyes was right. Perhaps I shouldn't practice medicine.

Jeff nodded. "Okay, let me slow up. When your mother left, it was an embarrassment. Faisal was humiliated, furious. When you left, it was an indication that he couldn't control even those close to him. It hurt his reputation. Do you understand? You're not to feel guilty over any of this."

"I understand, Jeff, but when it's you in that hot seat, it's hard to be so sure of yourself and feel guiltless."

"I get it, I really do. Anyway, I couldn't find anyone to talk with and none of my informants had news of Faisal or his men. The troops have been cycled through, for the most part, so the trail in Syria is cold. That said, I think your house proves that the trail is still there, but moved to the U.S. Not sure it's him, but I don't know why anyone else would target you like that."

"Will this never end?" I groaned.

"Most people wouldn't have survived this long, Sonia. I'm going to say this, and it's not going to make you happy, but I want you to think about it. Can you take it?"

I wondered what he could say but decided it was coming from Jeff, and he knew me well. "Go ahead."

"There is a stubbornness in the Emir. You're his blood. Your strongest weapon against him is what you inherited from him. Your intelligence, your ability to survive, and your determination to succeed. You two are warring factions because you stand for good, and he stands for evil. No one can take him out like you can." Jeff held my eyes with his own.

"Whew, what a burden you just handed me! Wow. I'm trying to take that in a good light." Jeff's comment made me tired and in truth, depressed me.

"And you should, because that's how it's meant. But think about it. All of us are looking for your father; we're judging him on the trail of murders and terrorism he leaves in his wake. But you, you, Sonia... you understand his mind, his psyche, and what makes him tick. Naturally, physically, you don't have a chance. You don't have the access or the backing that he has. He's also been on his home turf up to this point. But... if you were to tell me about him, about your life growing up... I mean *really* tell me, then together we may be able to take him out."

I thought about what he was saying, and unhappily, it made sense. "I get what you're saying, Jeff. I just don't know if I can go through that emotionally."

"What better way to exorcise your own demons than to stand and fight?"

That flipped on a light. I faced Jeff and nodded. "You're right, and I don't know why I didn't think of it that way in the beginning. He trained me to be the weaker sex but all along, as you said, I've been as strong as he is. I'll do it, Jeff—or die trying."

Jeff smiled at me. We were a team. And Tessa made three.

Chapter 11

Life turned a corner for me that day. Jeff had been right. I'd been running and hiding for long enough. I'd proven my capabilities. And what I was incapable of was far too apparent. I only had to look at my medical and military record to see that. I took a stand that day, and it colored my thoughts and my life differently.

I didn't say anything to Jeff yet. I asked him for some time. I wanted to try on the sensation that I was a warrior and not a victim before I committed.

Each day the Agents Smith came and went. Jeff came home with news, although most of it was small things. They were looking for the Emir's associates who were already in the U.S., hoping one would slip and lead the Agency to his whereabouts. I could have told him that waiting for my father to slip was useless. If anyone was careless enough to leave a trail, his own men would decapitate him— literally and figuratively. There could be no witnesses and no one to repeat the stories. It was a forever forward progression of training recruits, obtaining weapons, developing strongholds, and organizing in ways that hadn't yet been traced.

Jeff, Tessa and I settled into a routine. I researched through the general Internet, and Jeff got me clearance to get into some secret government information. We were, after all, on the same side. I cooked magical dinners which we shared in front of the television or just sat and talked about what we'd discovered during the day. At night we took turns in the bathroom and went to our respective beds.

I missed Paul, but Jeff kept me up-to-date on his medical status. Unfortunately, Paul never regained consciousness. There was rumor of a period of apnea, a four- or five-minute period-of-time when no air got to Paul's brain. No one seemed to know why he'd become apneic but I was convinced someone was responsible. I knew there could be a dozen reasons. I figured someone had stuffed a pillow over his head either in Germany, or shortly after we returned to the U.S. A pillow over anyone's face that long could easily cause brain damage. Not to mention someone slowed down his heart-beat with drugs to cause the heart attack. There was also the possibility of switching off his ventilator. A hundreds ways they could have killed the man I loved. My thoughts returned to the strange physician and nurse at Ramstein who no one knew. I realized these thoughts could be considered delusional and bizarre so I kept them to myself and shared them only with Jeff. There was hushed talk of a severe brain injury. But no one had said for sure. I heard they planned to start the brain function tests next week.

In the meantime, my daily routine continued. Tessa's exercise times were mainly at night and my protectors took her out several times each day. All in all, I was calm. There is a sense of security in routine; one that is sadly overlooked. In the instant gratification world we lived in, we don't stop to realize that at one point, it becomes our personal responsibility to provide that gratification. It gives us a feeling of restlessness and the denial of having accomplished a goal, for in our own minds, we just set the next one. We continually set our personal bars higher and I work to do this each day

Perhaps it was that routine that brought Jeff and me closer together in a different way than we had been. His role had been protector and handler during past years; mine had been an expert in both the medical field and in the languages and customs of the land that had been my home for so long. We'd been a good covert team. We'd worked together, but were never as intertwined as we were becoming.

I vacillated between fear and self-doubt, both instilled by my father, and the warrior woman inside who knew she alone possessed the power to lure him into the open and then slay him. That just led me back to the self-doubt. It was a vicious circle and one I could not escape.

We began a habit of watching the game show, *Jeopardy* every evening. We threw out answers and laughed at one another when we missed one.

It made us companionable. That night we finished an entire bottle of wine between us and then watched another episode of *The Sopranos*, our latest binge show. Jeff talked me into watching a second, making it later when I went in to bed.

I showered and slid between the clean sheets, puffing the pillows as I always did around myself. I thought how dogs seek a bed but first clear their spot of unfriendly bedfellows by walking in a circle and patting and scratching the bed with their paws. It was all I could do not to get down on my knees and look under the bed; I'd become paranoid since I found out my father was still alive!

I lay awake for a long while, thinking about the character Tony Soprano and how he managed to maintain respect in the face of constant take-over attempts. I suspected The Emir lived a similar life. He would have bodyguards to protect him while he slept, and even those could be bought off by someone wanting to steal the throne. His was a self-imposed life of jeopardy. There had to be something in that lifestyle that I could use to get to him. He was caught in something inevitable and yet chose to stay. Why?

I was standing on what I knew to be a deserted island with nothing more than a stick in one hand and nothing, not even clothing, to protect myself. Survival depended on my leaving the island and hoping that over the horizon was safety. I didn't know it to be there but had to have that faith because the alternative was certain death.

I took care to sharpen the stick, for around the island swarmed hundreds of sharks, each hungrier than the last. Somehow, I had to outwit them because they outnumbered me beyond belief. I squatted and watched the bigger ones nearest the shore. There was one who, while not the biggest, seemed to be the smartest. He had dead fish eyes like Milliken, but he was instead intelligent, chasing the others near him away as he swam in tight circles. I calculated my timing and then stepped into the middle of his circle. Now, his space had been invaded. He could no longer defend against the circling swarm and attack me at the same time. He had to make a choice. I had the stick, and I poked circling sharks in the eyes, making them bleed, and the others would set upon the new scent of blood. The leader shark moved consistently into deeper water; the pair of us leaving a trail of death behind us. Evil fed upon evil. Finally, we were in deep water. Now he had the advantage as he could swim without surfacing for long periods, while I had to keep my head above the surface and couldn't watch my feet. Then, he had me. At that point, he could become my protector, as I had been his, or he could swim away and leave me to the others. Or, he could eat me himself. I looked him straight in those black eyes and challenged him, and he came at me, mouth open. I reared back and thrust my stick into his mouth as hard as I could.

He flopped and fought, trying to dislodge it, but as he did, he bled more and more. Soon the others set upon him, tearing him to bloody shreds of shark flesh. And just as he had done, I calmly swam out of the circling frenzy and into clear water until I'd cleared the horizon to look for land. But, there was no land, and I couldn't go back. The sharks had learned my trick and now were circling me. Who would guard me?

"Sonia!" I jerked upright at the sound of a male voice nearby. "You were having a nightmare."

I nodded my head, tears rising, and I could feel my jaw quivering. Tessa stood at the side of my bed and licked my hand.

There were a few moments of silent thought, and then I felt the covers next to me being turned downward. Jeff's warm body slid in, and his arm pulled me against his chest. "I think it's about time we talk about your life and growing up."

"He was a shark," I sobbed.

"But you have the sharp stick," Jeff said softly, and my thoughts were filled with wonderment. How had he known?

Chapter 12

Looking back, I think Jeff may have been the only reason I survived. His support and empowerment introduced an entirely new perspective into my life. We changed our routine and began going to bed, in his room, together. We formed a rather strange relationship. Admittedly, it was strange but somehow it was comforting.

He understood I was engaged to a man who was not present and therefore couldn't fulfill the promises we'd made to one another. Jeff also realized that I was loyal, and even though he sensed I may be falling in love with him, he didn't press me to be intimate. We didn't want to ruin what we had with guilt.

I had come to realize that Jeff was everything that Paul had never been for me. He listened to my thoughts and didn't immediately over-ride them, as Paul had often done. Paul was, first and foremost, military and his behavior and conversations bordered on brisk. Jeff was far more of a process person, most likely based on a lifetime of studying behavior and spying. Jeff was also more masculine, and I needed an alpha male to maintain my own sense of balance in the relationship.

And so, we lay side-by-side, and he held me, smoothed my hair and kissed the top of my head.

He encouraged me to talk, and talk I did. I began with as far back as I could remember—when I was three. I told him how life had been when my parents were still together and then how my father had gotten caught up in the movement, and as he did, the more distant he became from us. His caring turned to control, and he was merciless to those who didn't follow his demands, my mother included. Jeff seldom interrupted and then only to encourage me to continue or to wipe my tears as the eruption of old memories caused pain and regret, not to mention fear. Tessa watched us carefully, as only a loving canine could, as our relationship blossomed. She was with us constantly and laid on the floor on what became my side of the bed. In my heart, I believed that Tessa approved of my relationship with Jeff. I hoped she did.

I no longer feared sleep and the nightmares because Jeff was next to me, interrupting their hold and surrounding me in warmth and caring until they were lost to memory. Perhaps even more importantly, Jeff taught me to fight back. He manned and encouraged my defenses. He helped me find strength and energy that I didn't know I had.

In my nightmares, I was always pursued. I never saw my pursuer, but I tried to outwit him. To jump high, to fly, to swim, to blend in with rocks—anything that would allow me to survive without conflict. With Jeff's encouragement, one night I finally took my stand. The pursuer was upon me and instead of hiding, two scimitars materialized in my hands. I began hacking it. Not just to behead it, but over and over until it was ground meat. After that, the nightmares stopped, and I was no longer afraid.

Jeff did these things for me because he cared. He cared because I knew he was in love with me. He couldn't hide it and really didn't try to. We both accepted it, and I knew I felt the same for him. But I had pledged myself to Paul and at times the guilt was overwhelming. But Paul wasn't there. He lay at Walter Reed, a mass of tubes, wires, machines and bandages. But still, I was regretful. What kind of woman falls in love with another man – when her fiancé lay critically ill, wounded by a bullet her father had ordered. Nevertheless, Jeff and I held ourselves to that code of honor, which was another reason we were well-matched.

One morning Jeff surprised me with breakfast in bed. "I think we've come a long way," he said, a smile on his face. "Your nightmares; they've gone, haven't they?"

My heart jumped for joy at my response. "Yes, ever since the one where I stood to face the enemy, it no longer has power over me." I was secretly pleased and couldn't believe the short amount of time it had taken me to slay my major dragon.

"That's what I hoped. Now we face the real one. I'm going to Walter Reed this morning and talk with the doctors. I want to make sure they're doing everything they can for Paul. I need to know what they believe his prognosis to be."

I nodded and looked down at the floor. I had known this time would come. I felt ashamed and hopeful at the same time.

Jeff touched my chin and I looked at him. "Sonia, it can't come as a surprise to you that your father would use Paul to hurt or lure you."

"Yes, I know he would. He has."

"Do you trust me, Sonia?" Jeff's hazel eyes searched mine.

"Of course."

"Here comes the hard one. It's my theory, and it's supported by investigative evidence that the untoward events, the "incidents" Paul suffered – and the reason why he remains in a coma - were attempts to kill him. You suspected that, didn't you?"

My eyes filled with tears. I nodded. "I was fairly certain. There were too many coincidences. There was no medical evidence to explain the apneic episode or his heart attack. Paul was as healthy as an ox. Even the extent of the injuries he sustained from the sniper fire couldn't and didn't explain a cardiac or respiratory event." I tried to be as professional and detached as I could, but we were talking about Paul. My Paul. The man I'd planned to love, honor and obey for the rest of my life. My resolve crumbled and tears streamed down my face. Jeff took me in his arms and comforted me.

"You're right, Sonia. "I also think they began back at Ramstein." Jeff hesitated. "In fact, I'm sure of it.

I agreed, my voice ragged from my tears. I wiped my eyes with my fists and wiped my hands on my jeans. "I think so too. That strange doctor and the head nurse. The two in Germany. Why is everyone so comfortable with that? Why aren't they suspicious?" I gulped. "That was when it began. That was when..."

"It's not their job to be suspicious, Sonia. It's their job to take care of their patients. You know this better than anyone. You're a physician. You're a healer. Medical staff have been trained to stay out of the politics of situations. Their jobs depend on that. But you... for you it's personal. It is difficult for you to become emotionally objective. Tell me right now. What is the most predominant emotion you feel when you think of Paul? Tell me truthfully?" He studied me quietly.

I held my breath, pretending to think, but I already knew. "Guilt," I whispered.

He nodded, although not with triumph. "That's what I thought. You're a good and honorable woman, Sonia. I know that if Paul was healthy, you would hold true to your commitment to him - if for no other reason than you *are* that kind of woman. That said, I know what I feel, and I'm reasonably sure I know *what* you feel. It's different between us and always has been. There has always been a love between us." Jeff gazed into my eyes.

I nodded but didn't speak. I didn't know what to say or how to say it.

"At first, I told myself it was the thrill of the game, so to speak. You could venture out into dangerous situations, meet informants, collect intel, sneak around the markets, because you knew I had your back. Paul was your safe person; the one who would permit you to do all that. Paul was safe, but he didn't necessarily fill the psychological aspect of what you needed, but were convinced you didn't deserve. Your father taught you that. You learned from him that what you wanted didn't matter. It's what the male wants that will prevail. That's typical Mid-Eastern culture for men like Faisal. That idea put you in conflict with Paul because, to you, he represented male dominance. Without his having done a thing, Paul became the ghost of what your father demanded of you. Do you see that?"

Thoughts rumbled into my mind. My brain was pelted with possibilities. He was right and I'd never realized it. The realization freed me. I'd been consumed with guilt about Paul. "Oh, Jeff, now that you say it, I see you're right. It makes sense to me. When did you get to be so smart?" I grinned at him. It was an awkward moment for us.

Jeff laughed. "I'm not smart. Just a survivor. I survive by reading people, and you know I care about you. You know very well that I risked having you and Paul go off into the sunset together and yet I'm willing to feel that pain just to be here with you now and to help you through this.

I began to feel a new ache inside; the ache of longing. Jeff was right. Things would never work out with Paul because I had him framed in my mind and in our relationship to prevent it. In truth, *Paul was nothing like my father, but in my mind, I had empowered him* to be the alpha, and so now I felt lost. At least until Jeff opened the new door.

But, as Jeff had pointed out, I was a woman of honor. I couldn't desert Paul while he was in this condition. Certainly not when he was sick. Perhaps, one day when he was whole again, we could examine where we were, and things would change. There was also the fact that he'd suffered a traumatic injury to his brain and people were known to emerge from their comas with changed personalities. I supposed he had brain activity, but I didn't know for sure. Otherwise, I believed the Army would have considered taking him off the ventilator. I didn't know what the future held, but I did know I was behaving in a manner that took nothing from my integrity. At least for now.

Chapter 13

"I want to see Paul," I told Jeff one morning a week or so later. "I need to see him, to let him know I'm still out here."

"I understand, but are you willing to take the risk?" Jeff surveyed me with cool eyes.

I nodded. I had to see with my own eyes how my fiancé was doing. Could my voice wake him up? Could I assist Colonel Grayson out of his coma? "Yes. I'm sure. I can't remain captive here forever. I appreciate all you've done in dealing with the insurance company and the re-building of my house, but enough is enough. Let me go to Walter Reed tonight. I don't want to run into Milliken; I'm not ready for that quite yet. He's liable to pull my license the next time he sees me."

Jeff grinned at me. "Milliken won't be a problem at this point. We have a cover story for you." Jeff looked at me out of the corner of his eye. "But, you're gonna have to deal with him and do what he says if you want to practice medicine."

I cursed under my breath.

Jeff shook his head. "Truthfully, Sonia, I think Dr. Milliken is on your side. He doesn't enjoy yanking high ranking officers', even retired officers', medical licenses. People oversee him and his practice as well."

A flash of anger burned my eyes. "So, you think I need to play the game." I knew my voice was tinged with sarcasm.

Jeff locked eyes with me. "Yeah, I do. And, the sooner the better."

"So, I have to pay the piper so to speak."

"Yes, you do. You need to get it out of the way. In these past few weeks, you made marvelous strides toward emotional safety. You can work with Fish Eyes." He paused, "Do you want me to handle it? Do you want me to speak with him?"

I shook my head. "No, Jeff, this I'll handle on my own. If I'm legitimately not in a good place, then I shouldn't be practicing. But, to tell you the truth, after all our talks, I'm feeling much better. I know there will still be times when I hear a loud noise, and it takes me back, but everyone has mental cues that remind them of things. The important thing is I'm still a doctor, still on the payroll at Reed and my leg is healed. I can walk without the cast, so I need to get in and have it removed. It's time I moved on."

"Don't be in such a hurry, huh?" He gave me his lopsided grin.

"I know…" I understood. We were on a plateau with our relationship. We both wanted to take it to the next level, but we'd agreed to remain apart until Paul was fit to be a part of the consideration.

"No, really. If you need to go in to Reed to get the cast off and see Paul, I think that's fine. I'll have someone watching you. But come home to here; stay here while you plan what you're going to do." *And until we see what happens with Paul, he wanted to say, but didn't.*

I nodded. The next morning, Jeff left first and when he came home that night, after dark, he went out again. This time he drove me in to Walter Reed. I went first and had a colleague remove my cast. He fitted me with a heel boot, and it felt great to be somewhat normal again.

Then I went to see Paul. He had slipped, so much that it took my breath. His color was paler, but that was to be expected as his Syrian tan faded. There was no color in his cheeks or his nose. His lips were colorless and stiff to the touch. His wounds had healed, and the bandages had been removed. He simply lay there, deep in his coma. According to the physician on duty, his brain tissue was much less swollen, so there wasn't nearly the amount of pressure on his brain. But it made no difference. Repeated brain scans indicated no brain function. Paul was brain dead. I couldn't get him to respond to my touch, deep pain stimulus or my voice, even when I shouted. My eyes clouded with tears. He'd been through so much and none of it should have happened. In my professional opinion, the added attacks, the unexplained cardiac arrests and periods of no breathing had taken a toll too significant for him to heal from.

I asked whether Paul's family had been contacted. He had a brother somewhere in California who didn't stay in touch with the family, and an uncle I'd never met. Otherwise, he was alone. I'd been his family, but I had no right to make decisions regarding his future. I was told that phone messages had been left, but no one had returned calls. So, it appeared, Paul was completely alone. That made me even more sad. Paul Grayson was a patriot, a decorated American hero. He was a military commander, a leader against the enemy, a selfless and brave man. But he had no one except me to mourn for him. Oh, perhaps there were a few enlisted men out there, but basically it was me. How sad was that?

"Hello, Dr. Amon." I whirled, surprised at the voice in the otherwise empty room. There stood Ester.

"Hello again, Ester." I appraised her with my eyes.

Ester's voice was professional. "I've been assigned to accompany you home. Mr. Hansen has been called away for a few hours."

"Oh?" I thought it strange that Jeff didn't text me and let me know himself. "Let me just use the bathroom and I'll be with you."

Once in the bathroom, I pulled out my phone, muted it and quickly texted Paul.

Ester here to take me to the apartment. Okay?

DELUSION PROOF

A few seconds later came his response.

Caught in a meeting. Yes. See you there later. I'm hungry for meatloaf. I smiled to myself.

I emerged from the restroom, took one more look at Paul and followed Ester to a small sedan with military plates. I sat in the passenger seat, and we exchanged only minimal conversation as she drove me to Jeff's apartment. Once there, she came upstairs and took up guarding the door. I let myself inside and lay down for a nap, shaken by what I'd seen with Paul. I needed time to process what I was going to do next. I fell into a fitful sleep.

When Jeff came home, I had his meatloaf waiting. "Go wash your hands," I instructed in my motherly tone. Without too much argument, Jeff had agreed to let me add one furnishing to his sparse apartment; a small table and two chairs for dining. We set it by the window where we could watch the skyline as we ate in the evenings. I'd set the table with two settings of Danish modern china in black, edged with slices of silver and two goblets with a wine cooling in a nearby bucket. I knew Jeff had eaten more meals out of a sealed container on a desert than he had in a fine dining room, and I wanted to make a difference. I peeked out and Agent Smith was here. Ester was gone. Jeff had evidently dismissed her for the day.

Jeff stood in the doorway of his bedroom, watching. His face shone, and his hair was slightly damp where he'd used a wet comb to tame it into place. "Would you pour the wine?" I asked him. He nodded and crossed the room to the table. I went back to the small kitchen and brought side dishes of fluffy mashed potatoes, green beans, a light gravy and a fresh fruit salad. I set these down and took my seat.

"I should come home more often," he quipped and that made me smile. It seemed I had discovered the joys of being a woman in a domestic role.

As if he read my mind. "Do you like this?"

"This?"

"Nesting, my mother used to call it."

I nodded and smiled. "Actually, it's bringing out a new side of me I hadn't realized was *wanting* out."

"It's very becoming," he complimented me and that pleased me again.

"Paul..."

He interrupted me with a flick of his hand. "Sonia, let's save that for after dinner."

I nodded, confused. Jeff poured the wine and I sipped the pungent liquid, letting it roll around on my tongue before I swallowed. Among many other things, my transition to a more civilian life had introduced the grace of doing things slowly. It made every gesture somehow more significant, more poignant. As a busy physician in my position, life up to that point had been more of a jet runway; setting up mobile hospitals, patching up the troops and getting another jet into the air and starting over again. This pace felt more appropriate and it also suctioned some of the urgency from my living in constant fear.

Jeff studied me. I felt his eyes watching me. "What are you thinking?"

There was that dreaded question that I'd been trained to avoid. As a physician, thinking often was nothing more than scientifically calculating an outcome and that led to false hope or dire expectations. As the daughter of a terrorist, I wasn't permitted to think, much less share my thoughts. They simply did not matter and were sure to lead to a misstep that would cost me. I wound my long, dark hair around my hand and brought it forward over my shoulder in what was now a thoughtful gesture. So many new facets of myself were beginning to surface.

"Actually, it was in my mind that I've been changing."

"Changing? How so? I mean, I see a difference, but I'm curious what you're seeing?"

"Oh, it's hard to explain unless you've walked in my shoes, but I suppose I could say that the early years of my life were relatively happy until *he* became involved in ISIS. I can even remember him being kind, if you can believe that. Then, when my mother was gone and I was alone with him, I lost my sense of self. Once I'd escaped, the sense of discipline kept me from thinking too much. The discipline worked and the routine held my emotions in check. Thinking can be a destructive force when you don't have the ability to change your circumstance.

Jeff watched me carefully. He nodded.

"Now, here I am, retired—a little more than I'd prefer at the moment, but nonetheless I don't answer to an alarm clock. That has given me a new perspective in how to spend the time; how to use it with grace and as a luxury." I hesitated. "I...I think it's a good change." My voice was hesitant.

"You *have* changed, Sonia."

"Then there's you, Jeff. You've inserted a funnel into the maelstrom that was my former self and allowed me to push it all out into the room without fear of reprisal. You've ostensibly let the cow out of the pasture!" I grinned at him. "I can barely remember a time when I wasn't following orders. You might say I've discovered my feminine side."

"Now *that* is the Sonia I've begun to see, and I like her, very much. Look at this meal we're enjoying. Sure, you cooked before, but not comfort food and certainly not from scratch. You know what else?"

I looked up with the curiosity of a child, hungry for praise.

He picked up his goblet and held it toward me in a toast. "You're glowing. I don't think I've ever seen you more feminine, more fulfilled. It's quite becoming."

I laughed; a sound I hadn't heard from myself for a long time. I raised my goblet to tap his and we both drank the nectar of self-satisfaction. I could see that it meant a lot to him to have had a hand in the transformation I was feeling. That turned my line of thinking. "Do you have news of my mother?"

He chuckled. "Melody is quite content, I assure you. She has always adapted well and right now she's the queen of the five-star resort." He paused. "I'd say she's loving life."

Smiling, I nodded in agreement. "Yes, she's like a chameleon. You don't know how often I wished I could be more like her. Less serious and more flexible."

"You *are* like her, you just don't realize it. You just never let it show."

We ate in companionable silence, savoring flavors and the illusion that life was good and secure. I wondered why I couldn't let that moment be just that—good and secure. Why were my worries always anticipated? I prepared ten steps ahead and then there were always another ten steps. I never let myself pause and enjoy the moment, as I was doing now. "I have cherry cobbler for dessert."

"Oh, no, now I *know* I'm in the wrong apartment. The Sonia I know doesn't know the difference between a cobbler and a cheesecake."

"Oh, I do so! With the cheesecake, you spoon the cherries over the top, like a sauce!"

Jeff found that exceedingly amusing as he helped to stack the dirty plates and move them to the sink. He brewed the coffee as I dished out the cobbler. We'd developed a very cozy, domestic rhythm, just the two of us.

We took our dessert to the sofa and fell against the cushions. "Can we talk about him now?" I asked in a subdued voice.

"Of course." Jeff nodded, sipped from his mug and waited. I took a bite, swallowed it as I prepared my opening line and then set my bowl on the coffee table.

"He looks bad, Jeff. Those episodes, of "accidents" or attempts on his life - whatever happened, took their toll. I haven't seen all the test results, but my guess would be that he's only hanging on because the plug hasn't been pulled."

Jeff nodded. "So, I'm told, Sonia."

"Really?" I gasped, my eyes filling with tears as I saw the confirmation in his face. It was one thing to think Paul wouldn't recover but another thing to actually know others believed the same.

"I've been waiting for the moment to bring this up. According to the physicians overseeing his condition, they don't believe recovery is possible."

I twisted my head and looked upward, attempting to restrain the tears that wanted to choke me. I'd known it in my soul and my brain had recognized it, I just hadn't wanted to admit it. Eventually, I nodded, but said no more. I just couldn't talk.

"Sonia, they're wanting to move Paul to a long-term care facility until they've located his family. I know you gave them what you know, but for some reason, they're not responding. There are certain provisions under the law in cases like this. You should also know that Paul has opted to be an organ donor."

I shook my head and waved him silent, full sobs surfacing as the words I'd said so many times to others, now applied to me. Jeff had been prepared for a breakdown, having scooted closer to me on the sofa and now enveloping me with his arms. When I had calmed somewhat, he went on. "As much as I don't want to say this, I think it's best that Paul be moved. Faisal is alive, as you and I agree. If not in body, he is in spirit and that spirit has been picked up by his followers. As you know, their fanaticism requires that they punish offenders. It may be that we're not dealing with your father, but those who will exact revenge on his behalf."

I nodded through my tears, using a tissue from a nearby dispenser to dab at my eyes. "That's occurred to me, as well."

"If that's the case, we may be chasing shadows and that could account for why we can't pick up a trail. My thinking is that whomever is after you, and possibly your mother, is using Paul as bait."

I jerked at those words as it made Paul's attack directly my responsibility.

Jeff knew what I was thinking. "No! Don't go there. This isn't about you—it's about Faisal and/or his disciples. You didn't provoke this; you never have. If anything, you've walked a line between sacrificing your own blood and helping to kill him. That can't be a good place to be, no matter how evil he is."

I shook my head. "Not as hard as you might expect. You haven't personally experienced his idea of family." I could feel bitterness welling up in me again and paired with distress for Paul, my heart was starting to race. I pushed away Jeff's arms and jumped to my feet, going to stare out the window. "I can't take it anymore, Jeff. I'm at my breaking point with all this."

Crossing my arms over my stomach in a self-comforting pose, the words poured out. "Maybe you've unleashed a dragon at the same time from me, I don't know. I've never felt such resentment as I am at this moment. What have I done to deserve this life-long, ongoing terror? Be born to the wrong man? I became a doctor so I could right his wrongs; can't you see that? I didn't want to admit it to myself, but it's true. I wanted to heal the hurt I couldn't fix in myself. That want led me to a frenzied need to heal others. Beginning with my mother. It is I who have become the parent and she the child. My mother is like my child. That's normal as people age, but not this early in her life."

I turned and faced Jeff. "No matter what this makes you think of me, I'm done. I am no longer his daughter. I am no longer paying penance for his sins. I am Sonia Amon, doctor and woman and... and..." I dissolved and the long-submerged cry of denial surfaced. Panic was overcoming my ability to think and as a ball of emotions, all I could do was pace the room, each round more frenetic than the last.

Jeff watched me and suddenly sprang from the sofa, his role as therapist done and his role as savior beginning. He strode into the kitchen and retrieved a bottle of whiskey from the cupboard over the refrigerator. He handed me a shot glass. "Drink this."

I pushed it away. "No, I'm too upset."

"That's why you're going to drink it. Don't argue."

I'd heard that voice too many times. It steered me through danger when discovery would have meant the end of my life. It steered me through horrendous explosions with body parts littering my feet as I tried to navigate the heavy smoke and poisonous air of the battlefield. It had been a beacon through some of the worst times in my life.

So, I did what I've always done when it came to Jeff. I trusted—and drank.

Jeff picked me up and carried me into the bedroom, laying me tenderly on the covers. His strength and warmth became my cocoon and he let me cry—so hard that it felt as though part of me would come loose inside. His hand smoothed the hair off my brow and he kissed my forehead, his lips smoothly sliding down my temples to kiss the sides of my nose. His deep voice cooed softly, telling me to let it out and that everything would be better, that he would see to it. Kissing my throat, my neck and whispering the words to a childhood lullaby into my ear.

I wanted him. I turned my face and received his kisses, returning them with a fervor of pent up emotion and need. Sonia, the woman, the child, the needy yet strong female gave in to passion and I wrapped myself around his neck and pressed my breasts into the muscle of his chest.

"I want you, too, but later, when this is settled," he whispered wisely. I nodded, but I didn't let go. God help me, I needed to be a woman, *his* woman, that night.

Chapter 14

I strode into Walter Reed and headed straight to my office. Frances, with her usual precognition was waiting with a cup of coffee and my favorite cheese Danish. If Walter Reed did only one thing right, it was to bake those cheese Danish.

"What's on my agenda?" I realized my voice sounded curt.

"Good morning to you too, Major Amon." Frances glared at me over her half-glasses. "Nothing is on your agenda. I left it open until you were ready to start up."

I was pleased. "Good. Call Milliken and get me in there, this morning, if possible." My voice was firm and I was resolute. I was going to end this cat and mouse game with Fish Eyes.

"Yes, ma'am!" Frances turned to leave but stopped. "Welcome back, ma'am."

I looked up and smiled, but it was strength that she saw. The worn down, frightened Sonia was gone.

I pushed back my chair and was on my way to talk to Paul's doctors. Frances intercepted me. "Dr. Milliken says he has time right now if you aren't busy."

Good! First things first. "Tell him I'm on my way."

I knew I was exerting a new energy because Milliken's face flushed and he stepped backward, out of my way, as I marched into his office. I set aside the preliminaries. "What do I need from you to resume practicing?"

Taken by surprise, he actually stuttered. "Well, I suppose I need to come to the conclusion that your PTSD will not arise at an inopportune time."

"I see. First of all, may I suggest that there *is* no opportune time for PTSD. It comes when it comes. Secondly, would you say you are capable of treating it?"

He nodded. "Yes, I'm qualified."

"Good, then you agree that it is treatable. I'm not referring to your treatment specifically, but you agree that it is treatable. Particularly when the individual involved is a licensed, highly-trained, medical clinician who understands the triggers and treatments. Would you agree?"

"I suppose, yes." Fish Eyes ogled me.

"Third, have you witnessed any behavior that would suggest I am incapable of resuming an active practice?"

"Witnessed? No."

"Then Dr. Milliken, you are wasting the skills and abilities of a trained physician by restraining me from practice. The government pays me to do my job and I'd like you to sign the appropriate documentation so that I may return to it. Any problem with that?"

I knew I was intimidating. I intended to be. I knew how to push his buttons and he no longer scared me. How could anyone scare me after what I'd been through?

As if in a daze, he nodded and opened a drawer, extracting a file folder. He signed the paperwork, gave me a signed copy and added another to my records. He looked at me and said, "I must insist you work through this PTSD treatment course and see me a couple of more times." He handed me an envelope.

I nodded and accepted the packet of information. "Done. Thank you. I'll be on my way," I said, concluding the meeting. He may have been a fine psychiatrist when it came to many conditions, but I was not his patient any longer, or at least not in my mind. He had nothing over me and had ceased to be a threat.

To my surprise, Frances was waiting outside the elevator when I left to see Paul. I handed the doctor's release to her. "Please see to it that this gets to whomever needs to see it. I'm picking up my stethoscope, Frances, and God help anyone who gets in my way."

"Yes, ma'am!" She saluted me and the pep had been restored to her step. Frances respected and loved assertiveness if it was according to code.

I sought out Paul's physicians by talking to the nurses at the monitoring station. I verified what Jeff had shared about Paul's prognosis and although they weren't obliged to do so, they shared all his test results with me. It choked me to say it, but I agreed with their opinion. I was hoping there was something they'd missed, as arrogant as that may have been. I was holding out for hope.

"Have any of his family members been in touch?"

Each of them looked to one another and the consensus was negative. I nodded. "What is your treatment plan?"

Dr. Denner, a very highly-respected physician who had been through Viet Nam at Walter Reed cleared his throat. "Colonel Grayson had signed a DNR which only recently surfaced. Part of his papers, records and identification had remained in Syria where he was stationed. I'm not certain of all the particulars, but his signature has been verified. I don't need to tell you what this means."

My breath caught in my throat. Many hospitals, including Walter Reed, suspend DNR orders during surgery when the patient is unable to breathe or when their heart fails to beat due to the actual medical procedure and not a bodily failure. The recuperative process is treated differently. Paul was no longer in the surgical unit. Paul was no longer an acute surgical patient. His wounds had healed. His brain activity was minimal to non-existent. It was precisely the type of situation for which a DNR was intended. Paul was ostensibly a nursing home patient. In fact, situations like Paul's were the reason for Do Not

Resuscitate orders. I knew Paul wouldn't want to live like this, his body living only because it was attached to a machine that was plugged into the wall.

They were obligated to remove mechanical life support and Paul's body would be called upon to fight or fail on its own.

I felt like I was choking. "When?"

"We've sent another round of inquiries out to the family members, stipulating the seriousness of the situation and giving them 72 hours from date of proven receipt to contact us. That will be up at 1600 hours, tomorrow."

I staggered. In a little more than one day, Paul would most likely die. Not a soldier's death on the field, not after a man's right to fight for his life, but at the hands of an unknown assassin who had been most likely armed and dispatched by my own father. The complexities were overwhelming, and I could feel my newly-discovered strength and resolve slowly beginning to dissolve.

"I understand. Please keep me posted."

Dr. Denner nodded and I left. I locked myself in my office and Frances locked hers to prevent anyone coming in. I cried and she held me, rocking me like a mother with a sick child laying its head on her shoulder. We talked about Paul; she'd known him well. We reminisced and even laughed. It was good. It was healing. It was all we had. We'd both loved him and tomorrow he'd be gone.

JUDITH LUCCI

I was present that next day at 1600 hours when my fiancé, Colonel Paul Grayson, my tall, blond, sometimes quirky fiancé was disconnected from all artificial means of maintaining his life. He was pronounced dead with no sign of brain activity eight minutes later. My soul was crushed. Frances stood by me and willed me strength through the short span of time.

I watched as the attending physician signed his death certificate and stayed until they came to remove his body. Standing in the doorway of his room, I watched until the gurney entered the elevator at the end of the hall. I watched as the doors closed. I had just watched the end of the first half of my life. If I was so lucky.

The next day, Jeff and Frances stood with me as we attended the ceremony at Arlington. The gun salute startled me. Jeff took my hand more firmly. He knew—he always seemed to know. In attendance were only a few people and none of them were family. I had a great respect for family, having such a convoluted, distorted example of my own. I laid a dozen red roses on his casket, their color patriotic when placed against the red, white and blue.

Paul was gone. I was moving forward into unknown territory and I had my mother to protect. I wouldn't go alone – and I wouldn't go in with anything other than courage and a commanding attitude. That much I knew. And in my court, I had Jeff and I had Frances. I considered myself lucky.

DELUSION PROOF

PART 2

Chapter 15

Military personnel are a varied group. Some were on the ground, pushing through the smoke and grenades to fulfill their orders. Others, like me, had their backs when injury interrupted the battles. Even now, I have their backs, although in a more remote sense. One thing we all had in common, though, was the need to keep facing forward. There was no luxury of looking over your shoulder while you were in the armed forces.

Now, it was my turn. I'd fulfilled my orders, survived my injuries, honored my dead; but now it was time to move forward. I suddenly realized that first morning I was due to go on duty—I had no idea how to do that.

There was a car waiting for me when I got downstairs from the apartment I was still sharing with Jeff. Just like my job, my relationship with him was filled with questions but luckily for me, he was a patient man.

As I approached, the door opened, and I saw that Ester was my driver for the day. She opened the back door, and I slid inside. "Good morning, Agent Smith," I greeted her. They were right. As long as I was to be under the protection of a bodyguard, making them all be an Agent Smith simplified things for me. She murmured something curt and closed my door, suddenly appearing before the steering wheel like a dark wraith that continually floated about me. *Would I ever know privacy again?*

My leg was completely healed. Fish Eyes Milliken was now pretty much in the past, and even my distant supervision of Paul was no longer needed. He was now watched over by the sun and the sky.

Even so, I felt incomplete and sickly. I knew it was likely to be a facet of the depressive side of PTSD, but I refused the medications due to their multiple side effects and inconsistent relief. I needed to maintain a clear head to do my job properly. I had, however, completed my PTSD modules from Fish Eyes and had to admit some of the coping strategies were helpful.

My mother, the ever-lovely, always sweet, yet vulnerable Melody, had refrained from joining me at Paul's funeral. She was still safely ensconced at White Sulphur Springs. The Agency felt the less she came into the public eye, the better. Her safety was paramount to me, so we accepted the distance and tried to fill it with speaking in Facetime, both our faces holding worry and the need for one another's side by side company. Were we destined to forever be in protective custody? Could we ever prove the Emir was really gone? Perhaps that was the real terror he intended; to forever live in fear. I took some pleasure in knowing my mother was happy at the five-star resort.

I also accepted that I was grieving for Paul. We never had the conventional house, two cars, and a family dog; but we'd had a sort of life together nonetheless. My relationship with Jeff was different. It bore no resemblance to that with Paul, other than they centered around duty and obligation.

Jeff had chosen the role of protector for the time being. He had access to the manpower, information, and inside intelligence that made all the difference. It was frowned upon for the two of us to be anything other than professional, but I dared anyone to step forward and try to separate us. We were a house of cards; Jeff, my mother and I. Smiling to myself, I added Frances to that list. She'd give me a stern lecture if she knew I'd left her off. We gave one another mutual support and shared the secrets we couldn't share elsewhere. There was solace in that, at least.

It felt good to walk the bright halls again once I'd arrived at the hospital, my shadow close behind. At first, I tried to be friends, to develop a rapport. None of the Agent Smiths had been receptive to friendship, least of all Ester. Jeff cautioned me it was better to keep things on a professional level, reminding me that any of the female agents could be called upon to save my life. They needed their unemotional clarity of thought to be the most effective.

"Good morning, Frances," I greeted her, wishing I could at least hug her. I needed a hug.

Frances was business-like as usual. "Dr. Amon. It's good to see you back. I've prepared a list of appointments for you, and you'll find it on your desk. Nothing too strenuous for your first day back." She straightened her collar as though she was about to undergo inspection. She plucked an imaginary piece of lint off her navy-blue skirt. I noticed she had on her pearls and I wondered what that meant.

"You shouldn't spoil me, Frances. Everything is healed, and work is the best medicine for what ails the heart."

"I could have told you that," she huffed.

"Oh? When did you get your medical license?" I teased her.

"No license needed for that, ma'am. Just good common sense."

I'd heard that phrase from her before. I had to admit that as long as I'd known her, Frances had never taken a day off sick. I wished I could say the same. My stomach had been upset in the car on the way to work, and I found the need to run to the bathroom off my office when I got in. I was in GI distress. I was flowing from both ends.

"You should have stayed home. You're not ready for this yet," Frances observed. It didn't pay to point out that what I did in the bathroom was private—she believed anything I did was her responsibility.

"I'll be fine. Call supplies and order me some masks and sterile gloves. If I've caught a bug, I don't want to expose patients." Although I wouldn't let on, I wished I had taken Frances' advice and stayed home. The bed and a cold cloth over my eyes sounded very inviting at that moment.

Frances frowned as she placed the order, and when it arrived, she slapped it on my desk a little louder than was necessary. "You're not helping, you know," I commented.

"Didn't intend to. Let me call your driver, and why not take another week off?" She smirked at me.

"Frances, we aren't quitters. I've spent enough time laid up. I need to work."

She didn't argue, but the door shutting and the overly loud mumbling she made sure I heard, drove her point home.

I masked up and headed to an exam room to see a patient who was coming in for a follow-up visit following his return from the Middle East. I was standing next to the exam table, using my stethoscope to listen to his heart when I felt my own heart beat erratically. Drawing back, I told the patient he sounded great and could get dressed. I quickly stepped into the next room and shut the door, listening to my own heart rhythm. Something wasn't right, but I assumed, given my other symptoms, that I'd picked up a nasty bug. I waited until I heard the door of the exam room next to me open and then gave him time to leave. Walking out, I headed toward my office but had to stop at a restroom along the way.

"Call my driver, would you, Frances? I don't think I'm going to be able to finish my schedule. You were right, and don't think it doesn't pain me to admit that right now."

She already had the phone in hand and came toward me, a small trash can in her hands. "Here, use this until I can get you a basin. Would you like me to get another doctor in here to look you over? Maybe prescribe something?"

"No, not necessary. I'd just like to get home. If I need something, I'll call." I took the can from her and noticed my fingers tingled as they touched the hard, metal rim of the can. For once, I was glad Agent Smith was lurking in the wings, even if it was the surly Ester. "Bring the car to the entrance, please?" She nodded and disappeared.

Frances appeared in the doorway. "I think I should ride with you."

"Don't be silly. I have the driver with me."

"Don't trust her. Haven't since I met her." She glared at me. "I don't like her. I don't like her *at all*." Frances gave me her stubborn look.

"Frances, you're letting your imagination run away with you."

"*My* imagination doesn't do that," she informed me sternly, and I managed a tepid smile.

"I'll be fine," I argued. Frances relented but gave me her "if something happens, I told you so" look.

Once I was settled in bed, I asked Ester to make me a cup of bouillon and find some saltine crackers. I also asked for a pitcher of cold water and a glass. She brought them quickly. "Will you be okay? Should I call Jeff?" she asked, a frown on her face.

Was she actually concerned about me? "No, not necessary. In fact, someone might suggest that he sleep on the sofa tonight. I may be contagious." Ester nodded but otherwise, showed no expression. I remembered Jeff's advice and thought again that while it was a necessary situation, I would like my privacy back.

I drank a glass of water, but the crackers didn't look like I could tolerate them quite yet, so I only nibbled on half of one before falling into a fitful sleep. I know I had nightmares but couldn't remember their content when I awoke. I felt confused and could do little more than try to sleep it off.

There was something cool, and I moved toward it. "There you go," said a low voice.

I opened my eyes to a slit and saw Jeff, leaning over me with a cloth in his hand. I shook my head, pushed him away, and said, "No, you need to leave. You don't want what I've got."

"If I get it, I get it, but I'm not leaving you in here alone."

"Just some water, and then go away. You can leave the door open, but please, I don't want you to get this. It's miserable."

Jeff gave me water to sip and then sat by my bed. I could feel myself drifting off. I was happy to see, when I got up to go to the bathroom, that he'd taken my advice and was snoring on the sofa in the living room. He awoke at the sound of flushing and sat upright. "Are you okay?"

I lied. "Yes, feeling better. Go back to sleep." I did the same.

The next morning Jeff was in the room, feeling my forehead and taking my pulse. "I'm taking you in to be looked over."

I shook my head. "No, no, don't be silly. It's just a bug, and I feel better this morning. I'll stay in bed. I promise. It would be a miserable and unnecessary trip to get looked over. They'll just tell me what I already know."

"Here, I'm going to get you some fresh water. I have a meeting this morning I can't miss."

"Thank you, cool water would be nice. I'll be fine, Jeff. Really, I will. Go to your meeting. If I need anything, I have my phone, and of course the ever-present Agent Smith outside my door."

Jeff returned with a pitcher of cool water. "A different Agent Smith out there today, just so you know. I think you've grown a little close with Ester and you remember what I said about that."

"Yes, I know, I know. I do like Ester. Don't lecture me now, please? Let me just go back to sleep."

"Okay, but I'll be calling Agent Smith to check in on you every hour."

Inside I was smiling. Jeff was acting like a worried mother, fussing over me so. I still felt awful, but at least my stomach was empty so that part was over. As long as I continued to get in some fluids, I would be fine once the virus ran its course. I took a deep breath and turned to my side in the bed, noticing that I was having mild cramps in my calves. I needed to hydrate better, so I managed another glass of water before falling back to sleep.

It was early evening when the sense that someone was in the room caused me to open my eyes. Once they became adjusted, I saw that it was Jeff. His eyes had circles beneath, and I felt badly that I was putting him out of his bed. "You look sicker than me," I softly told him. "Maybe you should get a room at a motel for the night and get a good night's sleep?"

"How are you feeling?" he asked, ignoring my concerns and suggestion.

"Much better." I wasn't lying that time. I truly did feel better. I reached for the water, and he beat me to it, handing me a glass.

"Thank you," I whispered. "Sorry, but my throat is sore. Boy, this is one of the nasty ones. Hits you from every direction."

"I'm glad you're better. I'll leave you be. I'm on the couch. You want something to eat?"

"No, I have crackers. Tomorrow I'll feel much better, I'm sure."

"Sonia?"

"Yes?"

"Don't leave me, huh? I need you."

"What? Oh, Jeff, silly you. I'm not going anywhere for a very, very long time."

"I'm holding you to that promise."

I watched the sun rise and my back hurt from lying in bed so long. I got up and went into the bathroom, where things were, thank goodness, relatively back to normal. I tiptoed past the doorway and saw Jeff on the sofa. It was too early to wake him, so I eased the door closed and sat up in the bed to watch the news. I felt sick again as I saw it was flooded with the reports of a suicide bombing not far away in D.C. The bomber had managed to get through security with an arsenal strapped to himself, entering a mosque while service was being conducted. He'd shot two dozen people, and then when he was rushed by others, he pulled a strap and blew himself and the heroic worshippers to bits. Acid rose in my throat. The speculation was that a terror cell had moved to the local area and despite being in the seat of American government, it had, so far, managed to stay submerged.

I'd learned while serving that while people were generally killed in these events, it was the survivors who also paid a toll—in fear. There was never proof that the cell had been eliminated. I could identify with that walking on eggshells, and the reminder sent me back beneath the covers. I felt myself shaking and couldn't remember where I was. I closed my eyes, and soon, it passed. Pulling myself off the bed, I made it to the shower and turned the water on as hot as I could. It helped to make me feel cleaner and a calmer me pattered back to bed. There was a tap at the door, and Jeff came in, looking disheveled from his night on the sofa. "God, you look awful."

"Gee, thanks," he chuckled.

I pointed at the television. "Did you see it?"

His head turned to look, and he stiffened. "I've got to go," he burst and stepped into the bathroom to shower and shave in the space of about 30 seconds. He emerged, kissed me on the head. "Agent Smith is outside. I'll be in touch." Then he was gone.

Chapter 16

It was a day of horrors. Still weak and off my game, I remained in bed, transfixed by the images I saw on the television. They brought back memories. I fought the rising panic. It was all too familiar; the children without parents wandering around and the parents, looking stunned as they tearfully tried to find their children. No one should have to go through anything like that. A church should be a safe place.

Agent Smith was a new gal; I liked her immediately. She was more relaxed and friendlier, coming to sit on a chair next to my bed to watch the reports with me. I don't know if Jeff instructed her to do that or not, but it was a kind gesture. Anyone who knew me would know it would have a strong effect on my psyche.

I tried to phone Melody, but it went straight to voice mail. I knew she was fine, but thought she might be seeing the reports and reliving bad times, too. I needed to remind myself that even though my mother was frail and a bit damaged, she was still a resilient woman. I left a message on her voice mail but didn't hear back from her at all. I knew she was in protective hands and should anything be wrong, I would be notified immediately.

Agent Smith brought me some chicken broth, and by mid-afternoon, I ventured as far as getting dressed. I was waiting in the living room for Jeff, but he hadn't made it home, although he called Agent Smith once an hour for a report, as promised. She told him I was doing much better and slowly getting my strength back. I would wait until he came back and talk to him personally. I knew instinctively that he was somehow investigating and unable to talk to me about it on the phone.

Agent Smith and I pooled our talents, and after she ordered a grocery delivery, I sat with a pot before me on the coffee table and peeled potatoes while she chopped the beef for stew. Carrots, pearl onions, and sweet peas rounded out the vegetable contribution, and by the time Jeff came home, the fragrant, cozy aroma made the apartment far more pleasant than where he'd been throughout the day. He dismissed Agent Smith, saying he'd be home with me. She nodded, having just washed and changed the linens on the bed. Things were feeling normal again if such a thing was conceivable on such a day.

I contented myself with just a few bites and some sips of the thickened broth while Jeff downed two large bowls. "That was great!" he complimented, and I acknowledged with a nod. He knew I was waiting to hear what he could tell me and that he was delaying it until after dinner so

145

we could eat in peace. The TV set was on in the living room, and we were companionably on the sofa side by side as the media threw conjecture around in their blindness.

"Okay, how bad?" I started the inevitable conversation.

"Bad," he answered, his eyebrows rising to indicate his concern. "Sonia, we have to talk."

Holding out my hand, I stopped him. "I already know what you're going to say. It's him, isn't it?"

Jeff looked at me, pity in his eyes. He knew the destruction his words would cause me. Finally, he nodded. "It's possible. Just possible, mind you, not probable."

"Based on what?"

"There are always patterns. Construction, materials used, the dress of the bomber; you know all this."

I nodded in misery. "Do you think it has something to do with me? Is this a sign?"

His response was brief. "Possible."

I sat forward. "Then the Agency is acknowledging he's alive?"

He shook his head. "It's just one of many, many conjectures on the table at this moment. Could also be someone he trained; someone who would leave the same signature."

"Oh, sweet Jesus. Jeff, this is my fault!" My heart was heavy and I felt like my chest was caving in. For a couple of moments, an elephant stood on me.

He turned and pulled me to him. "No!" he answered firmly. "It's not your fault and never has been. If, and that's a big IF, this is him, he is the one responsible. Not you."

"You don't understand. My father never forgets, and he will extract his payment one way or another; even if it takes two lifetimes. His and mine. Oh, my God, Jeff. Melody! I haven't been able to reach her today!" I knew my voice sounded hysterical.

His hands on his knees, he hefted himself to a stand and grabbed his phone from the counter where he'd left it. He stepped out onto the balcony, and I watched his face in silhouette as he shouted into the phone. I grew cold and began to shake again. Jeff finally pushed open the slider and came inside. One look told him I was in trouble.

"Okay, so she's been locked in her room today, and no one realized it. There's so much to do there at the resort, and she generally golfs or swims. They went to check on her while I waited and had to break in her door."

I tensed, waiting for the words I didn't want to hear. "Jeff?"

"Sonia, she's fine, well at least she's safe. They're calling in a doctor, but the agent assigned to her said she appears to be in shock. Her television was on in the room, so my guess is, she

147

had a flashback. They're seeing to her now, and you know more about this stuff than I do."

"Call them back. I want a full report from the physician who examines her. Give them my direct number."

"Can't do that, Sonia. If it's him, they could be tracking your phones and triangulating locations. It's too dangerous. I'll tell them I'll call back in a half-hour and you can use my phone to talk to him. My phone is swapped out every other day, and it's safe."

I nodded and sat back, that awful dread seeping through me once again. I was the little girl again, waiting to hear the next punch and my mother's cries of pain.

Jeff sat with his arm over my shoulder as I continued to shake. "Look, I'll make us some tea."

I nodded but didn't answer. I knew he'd be all thumbs in the kitchen, but I couldn't help him. Not this time.

Where had all my resolve gone? One little stomach bug and the great Dr. Amon was rendered helpless again, crouched and mewling in her bed. What was happening to me?

Jeff came with the tea and practically forced it down my throat. I had to admit it helped warm me up and took some of the soreness away. "What's in this?"

"A little brandy is all."

"Good stuff," I commented, and a sense of balance began to return.

His cell rang. Jeff stood, and this time, he didn't go back onto the balcony. He told the person on the other end to put the doctor on the line and that I would be taking the call.

It seemed Melody had suffered some degree of a psychotic break. She'd detached from reality for the first time – or at least that was someone's opinion. My heart was broken. She'd never reacted this way. My heart died a little bit because I knew that she may never come back but my better judgement reminded she most likely would. But of course, it hadn't been that long ago that she'd been in his clutches and a game for his henchmen. She'd recovered from that, only because she'd thought him dead and the two of us safe. But, the monster had foiled us again. He was back and I don't think my beautiful mother would ever get over this. My heart cried for her. I thought of her delicate soft skin, her silky blonde hair and delicate throat. But most of all, I thought about the life of pain and misery she'd lived because of Faisal Muhammed, who was nothing but a murderous killer. I was the only little girl, the only teenager who ran away from a murderous father, and the only woman, a United States Army Major, to be a sworn enemy and daughter of an ISIS commander.

But I would make it. My mother might not.

The doctor advised that a nurse be hired to stay with my mother and to administer sedatives and a medication that could be effective to break

149

through to her. I seconded his recommendation, and he said he'd take care of the arrangements. I told him to give Jeff updates and to add Jeff to Melody's list of people to contact in case of an emergency.

I disconnected but wasn't sure how I felt. Melody had been through the Emir's torture so many times, and for so many years, there was no telling how deeply-seated her break had gone. With rest, therapy and medication, it was possible they could help her. I, on the other hand, was useless. It was frustrating, to say the least.

My mother had paid and would continue to pay the price. She'd pay until the day she died. He'd gotten to her and I didn't know if she'd recover.

My pained eyes sought Jeff's green ones. "I have to see her. She won't get better without me."

Jeff pressed his lips together and shook his head. "We can't do that, Sonia. It's too risky."

My eyes pleaded with him, but he remained resolute. "I will try to link you to her by a secure line." He shook his head. "That's the best I can do for now."

I nodded. I understood Jeff's position. My thoughts returned to Melody. I understood what she was feeling, and I knew I was powerless to help her.

I handed back Jeff's phone and was thoughtful and quiet as he flipped the news back on. I must have cringed because he smoothly changed channels and we were then watching *Casablanca*, one of my all-time favorites. It finally drew me out. "This is one of my favorite parts. He's letting her go even though he wants her to stay. It's hard to imagine that level of unselfishness."

"Is it?"

I was quiet. "I think I'll call it a day. It's okay to sleep in the bed with me now, if you like."

"I like."

Jeff turned off the lights, double-checked the door and windows and joined me just as I was checking my email on the phone.

"I thought they took that away from you?" he asked and pulled my phone from my hands. "It's not safe, Sonia. It can be tracked. It's like a homing device that leads straight to you."

I let him take it. "I didn't think," I muttered and sank down against the pillow. I wanted to scream bloody murder. My mother was ill, and I couldn't see her. I couldn't even talk to her, for God's sake. I felt like a prisoner.

Jeff looked at me and pulled me toward him. "Whoa, Sonia, nobody's mad at you. I'm sorry— didn't mean to trigger old reactions."

Tears burned my eyes. "No, I'm sorry. I shouldn't have over-reacted like that. You did nothing wrong. Take the phone and destroy it, please? Can you get me something? Like a throw-away? I don't want to be without one."

"Of course. Ester is on duty tomorrow. I'll have her bring a couple."

"Thank you." I stretched and hunkered down beneath the covers, closing my eyes and waiting for the images behind my eyelids to go away so I could fall asleep.

Chapter 17

I felt appreciably better the next morning. My throat was still sore, but tolerable. Ester, Agent Smith, came into my room after Jeff had gone. She had two phones for me and brought some oatmeal with blueberries on the top. I acknowledged her with a weak smile and a nod. She was always so stand-offish, but I really needed a friend. Just someone to talk to. I picked up the remote and flipped the news back on.

The images from the bombing were still blocking all the rest of the news. They showed bodies covered with tarps until the crime scene had been catalogued. Then would come the body bags and the ambulances that were almost sarcastically promising healing as they made their way to the funeral homes.

"How horrible," I said softly.

"It's part of life," she surprised me by answering. I seldom heard her voice. Her voice held no emotion.

"How do you deal with it?"

"With what?" Her eyes queried me.

"Well, your job. I assume you see death on a regular basis and it's needless and cruel."

"As you said; it's my job. I do it well. I've learned how over the years."

Her words made me incredibly sad. I likened Ester to an automaton. Someone without emotions or feelings who lives to work. I felt her life must be empty, barren. "Listen, would it be off protocol if you were to keep me company inside today? Maybe play a game of cards?"

She looked as though she was about to argue, but thought twice about it and finally nodded. "Sure."

"There's a deck in that top drawer." I pointed and she retrieved them. "Sit down. How about gin rummy?"

Her eyes widened and I realized she must not be a card player.

"It's okay, it's easy and I'll teach you."

She shook her head. "Not allowed."

"Oh, c'mon, Ester. The Agency won't care. You're right next to me. You can't protect me any better than that, can you?"

She shook her head again. "No, I can't. I can protect you inside or outside, but cards are a sign of evil."

I laid the cards down and leaned back against the pillow. The only explanation was that she'd been raised in a strict religion.

"Where are you from, Ester?"

She shook her head. "You wouldn't know it. Please, I must leave now," she gushed and hurried out of the room. I was puzzled by her skittish behavior. There was nothing warm or friendly about her. I knew the Agency was just an excuse.

She had something far deeper holding her back. I was curious, but I knew the Agency didn't take in marshmallow softies when it came to recruiting. She was hired because she was tough and likely very good at her job. I could deal with that. That said, I also remembered when I met her that she'd said she was from New York and that her parents were Turkish.

I sighed. I had enough to worry about without disassembling the mysterious Ester. That had already been done by the Agency and it was up to me to take care of myself, get back on my feet and somehow get to Melody. I knew it would be difficult and that Jeff would find a hundred reasons I shouldn't, but she had to be scared and I knew I was the only one who she could truly talk to.

Something was drawing me from sleep and yet I wanted to remain asleep because it meant I didn't hurt. But this pain was stronger than I was. My eyes opened and I ran for the bathroom. Again. Damn! It was back. Was I so weakened from the previous few months that a virus could just hang on and on? Had my grief for Paul wounded my immune system. I remembered reading an article recently in a medical journal about a stubborn gastrointestinal virus that lasted for weeks. I felt so bad, I didn't think I'd last for weeks. I had broken out in a huge sweat and my weakness had returned.

Once I stabilized, I headed back for the bed but leaned out the bedroom door and called out, "Agent Smith?"

The door opened and I heard her come in behind me as I crawled back into the nest of blankets and damp pillow.

"Yes?"

Startled, I looked around quickly and saw that it wasn't Ester at all, but the girl I'd liked earlier in the week. "Can you help me, please? The virus, the bug. It's come back on me and my sheets are soaked. I don't understand what's going on."

"Of course!" She went into the bathroom where the linens were kept and pulled out fresh sheets and pillow cases. I scooted into a nearby chair long enough to let her do her job and then gratefully crawled back. "Did the other Agent Smith leave?"

She nodded. "She called in to say she wasn't feeling well, so I'm filling in for her. Maybe she caught what you have."

"Oh, God, I hope not. It's nasty. You'd better wash your hands thoroughly and just put those sheets in a garbage bag. I'll order more online. I don't want you handling those any more than necessary."

"Oh, it's okay. If I'm going to get it, I'm already exposed. Let me pop these into the washer with some hot water and bleach and I'll be back."

I nodded and watched her leave the room, thinking how much friendlier she was than Ester. I'd just closed my eyes when it hit again and I made for the bathroom.

I smelled disinfectant and heard familiar sounds. I thought I was dreaming until I opened my eyes and recognized the ER of Walter Reed. "What happened?"

Jeff's face came into focus. "You'll be fine. Agent Smith found you face down on your way to the bathroom and called me. We brought you in. They're giving you fluids. You should know better, Sonia, after all."

"I'm going to take that as a loving criticism." If I didn't feel so bad, I'd be mad at Jeff. I wasn't a child.

"Dr. Amon," spoke up a doctor I'd never seen before. "I'm Dr. Clemmons; I don't think we've met but I've heard a great many flattering things about you. You're seriously dehydrated so we're obviously administering fluids and would like to keep you overnight for observation. I've added some Zofran so you should be feeling more comfortable soon. Now rest. You're *safe* here."

I nodded, but noted his emphasis on the word "safe." Was he intimating that I wasn't safe at Jeff's apartment? Certainly Paul hadn't been "safe" at Ramstein or at Walter Reed. What did he know? Too many questions. I'd wait until my head was clearer.

"We're moving you to a room now," Dr. Clemmons finished up. Halfway there, Frances appeared beside my gurney.

"Well, what have you gotten yourself into now?" she demanded. To Frances, illness meant you hadn't properly taken care of yourself and was a reason to be chastised. Frances only operated in dark black and pure white.

"Hello Frances. Not now, please? You can dress me down later."

"You may depend on that!" Frances and her sergeant's voice drifted away and soon I was between clean sheets and in an environment that was home to me. I knew finally I'd be on the road to recovery.

Chapter 18

"I *need* to go see her, Jeff. I won't take 'no' for an answer. I'm her daughter and I'm not going to live in fear any longer." I hoped my voice convinced him. I *had* to see my mother.

"Sonia. You know the risks." Jeff arched his eyebrows. He really didn't want me to go.

"I'm willing to take them."

Deep sigh. "Okay, I won't argue with you but you're not going alone. I'll assign you a driver who will look out for you."

"Whatever. I'm leaving at seven in the morning, sharp. I'm feeling much better now and I can't put this off any longer."

"I get it, I just don't like it." His face was stony. He must really think I was in danger.

I looked at Jeff with a hard stare. "I haven't liked any of it since the very beginning, you know."

"Do you think we've made it harder on you? Is that what you're saying?" His voice was caustic.

I was losing my patience. "I won't say there haven't been times that I felt like bait, if you want to know the truth."

"Not fair."

"Why."

"He's your father."

"And that makes me responsible for what he does?" I snapped. I was incredulous.

Jeff shook his head. "No, of course not. That's not what I meant. I just meant that you're best positioned to help us stop him."

"I think I've more than done my share. You guys take over from here. I'm going to live as normal a life as I can."

I turned over, my back to Jeff. I felt his hand on my hip.

"Don't be mad, Sonia. I know how hard this must be for you. Being sick so much has to drain you, and then not knowing what's up with Melody. I get it."

"I'm not mad. I'm just tired and determined. You can't blame me for that."

His hand patted me and then withdrew. "You're right. I can't. I guess you know I'm not comfortable having you out of sight."

I flopped over, staring at him even though it was dark in the room and he couldn't read my eyes; only my voice. "There's nothing comfortable about any of this, Jeff. Never has been. It was my fate to be born to him and it's your job to stop him. That's about all that can be said. Don't think I'm leaving to get away from you. Far from it. And don't think I won't miss you. I will—terribly. But this falls under family duty and I'm all the family she has."

"I know," he whispered and I heard the sadness of resignation in his tone.

I reached and my hand landed on his chest. "I won't stay long; a week at the most. I need to decide where she will be taken care of the best. To evaluate her and talk to her doctor. I need to do that in person. I'm daughter, doctor and caretaker, all rolled into one. You understand, right?"

"I understand."

I felt him move toward me and as he pulled me into his protective hug, his lips took over mine. "Be careful," he whispered.

"I always am."

I felt weak, but stable enough for the car ride from D.C. down to White Sulphur Springs, West Virginia. In fact, I was looking forward to it. It would be a welcomed break from my confinement in the bedroom and then the hospital. Jeff kissed me good-bye and went to work as I waited for my ride. My luggage was packed and sitting next to me, including my medical bag. I wasn't sure what I'd find. I was licensed to practice in West Virginia, but I'd leave that for her current physician. I planned to assess my mother and then confer with her doctor.

There was a knock at my door. I opened it to find Ester standing there. Confused, I said, "Yes?"

"I'm here to escort you to see your mother," she said in an unemotional voice.

"I don't understand. I thought—well, I was expecting a different Agent Smith is all. Hold on, would you? My bags are right on the bed. I'm going to make one last bathroom stop before we get underway."

She nodded and went around me to get the bags. I made for the bathroom, locked the door and called Jeff's number. It put me straight through to voicemail so I tried texting, but there was no response. I had to learn to trust him and not always take over. Maybe he couldn't get the other girl or maybe she'd gotten sick. Whatever the reason, I knew he would have tried to appease my wishes so I needed to be graceful about it. I covered my intentions by flushing the toilet and running the water in the sink before I came out. Ester was waiting.

"Here we go!" I announced as cheerily as possible and walked around her to go downstairs.

The fresh air smelled wonderful. I asked her to leave the window down as we drove, and she obliged by a mere one inch. "It's not regulation," she told me curtly. I made a mental note to ask Jeff for some guidelines on their regulation. It seemed the Agency operated under a completely different set than the rest of the government.

The Interstate seemed faster than normal but perhaps that's because I had grown accustomed to the slow back-ups in the city. I leaned back against the cushions and stared out the window as we began to rise in altitude.

White Sulphur Springs was a one-time secret resort buried high in the Smoky Mountains at the southern point of the range. At ground level was a magnificent, one-time five-star hotel with the old money look often used by health spas from the earlier part of the century. Boasting more than one golf course, horseback riding, swimming pools, tea rooms with string quartets and its very own airport, it was a destination for old money and wealthy politicians. Its secret lay in the underground bunker that had been built to house the president and others should we ever come under nuclear attack. It functioned as a second situation room, as found in the White House. Somewhere along the way, it had been decommissioned like an old war ship and now was still semi-functional but more powerful in lore than reality.

The resort aspect, with its foul-smelling Sulphur water springs was where Melody was staying. Its spa echoed those in Europe and although I'd only been there once, I had fond memories of fine dining where you dressed in evening gowns and waistcoats and expected polite conversation and impeccable service. I was looking forward to being pampered a little after what I'd been through.

Ester and I did not speak at all except for the most perfunctory comments such as my needing to stop for a ladies room or she to get gas. This appeared to be our *norm,* at least between the two of us. I knew she didn't behave this way with others because Jeff had spoken highly of her in every sense. He would never have tolerated her coldness toward me.

I tried not to let it bother me as we drew closer to our destination. I asked her to stop at a tiny shop built on to the side of someone's house. The woman who lived there was elderly and an accomplished quilter. She was offering them for sale as they hung from wooden dowels and the atmosphere made me just want to lie down and nap. I chose one in bright colors that I hoped would cheer up Melody. Despite the luxury of the resort, her confinement and fears were certainly not healthy for her.

We arrived and pulled up to the portico at the main hotel. Guest cottages dotted the grounds but I knew Melody would be in where there were others who could look after her. I checked at the desk and they directed me to her room.

The door opened to my finger tapping, so I pushed open the door and saw her sitting in a wingback chair, looking out the window with her back to me. "I'm here," I called softly.

Without a word, she turned in the chair and held her arms out to me. I hugged her and she laid her head on my chest like a child seeking to be comforted. I was always amazed at how tiny my mother was. In many ways, she reminded me of a fine, porcelain doll.

"It's okay," I told her softly in a reassuring voice. Tears spilled down her beautiful, but aging cheeks. She didn't want to let go, so I took her hands in mine and gently pulled them away.

"Mom, it's okay. It's me, Sonia. I'm here and we're both safe."

"Sonia, Sonia, I've missed you so much. I hear such horrible things," she whispered. Her blue eyes sought reassurance from me. "It's him, isn't it?"

"Shhh..." I stroked her blonde hair that was now fading to gray. I wanted to take her to the hair salon to get it highlighted. They would make her look and probably feel better. Her face showed the stress she'd been under and the light was gone from her beautiful eyes. My beautiful mother was wilting like a delicate rose whose time had come and gone. My mind sobbed as my heart continued to thud dismay through my body.

I heard a noise and looked up. Ester was standing in the doorway. For some reason, I felt furious. "Ester, please wait for me in the tearoom."

"My instructions are to stay with you."

I hugged my mother and stood up, walking out the door and waiting for Ester to follow. She stood in the doorway, staring at Melody. "Ester!"

She slowly turned her head to look at me, as if she was in a daze. "This is Melody?" she whispered.

Anger flowed through me. "Come with me, now!" I backed up and eventually Ester nodded and followed. "Look, I don't know what's the

165

matter with you, but she's not your responsibility and as of right now, neither am I. You take the car and go back to D.C. If Jeff has a problem with that, tell him to call me."

She shook her head. "No, ma'am. I answer to the Agency, not you."

I cocked my head as I stared at her. Who did she think she was? "Listen to me. I'm going to explain this to you one more time and then you will leave. You—Agent Smith—you work for the Agency but you've been assigned to me. In a military hierarchy, I outrank you so highly that you wouldn't be permitted at my table for a glass of water. Do you understand? Now, take the car and leave me here. I am taking over responsibility for myself. You are dismissed." I knew I was being rude and arrogant, but I didn't care. I'd decided I really didn't like Ester.

Ester stared at me, pulled the phone from her pocket and continued to stare at me as she made her phone call. She spoke only a few words but the person on the other end was very proficient at issuing orders. She nodded, tapped the phone dead and with a blank look on her face, she turned on her heels and walked toward the lobby, her steel-toed shoes tapping with military precision on the polished floor. I watched her go and then went back to Melody, Ester was flushed from my mind.

"Talk to me, sweet daughter," Melody begged, and I pulled a second chair close by, sitting and taking her hand. "I'm right here."

"Is it him?"

The question. It had haunted me. Even from the news reports, someone who knew what they were looking for, how he operated, could see the signature. It was, exactly, what the Emir would do. Melody, as spent as she was emotionally, could see it, too. We were both going through a simultaneous flashback and no one could help us. We could only help one another. I knew how miserable I was. I couldn't imagine what she was going through.

That's why I did the one thing I swore I'd never do.

I lied to my mother.

"No, it's not him," I told her and it felt like the heavens opened and the angels damned me to hell. I was leaving her unsuspecting, vulnerable. At the same time if I'd told her the truth, her hell would have begun in that moment and she would have run—far and never come back. That was what fear did to you. I wanted to run, but I had to stay. I had to protect her now that I'd taken away her caution—now that I'd lied.

As miserable as I'd been the previous weeks, the break at White Sulphur Springs was a welcomed relief. Melody and I became sisters, in a sense. I knew it was the conversion of roles, where the mother becomes the child. It happens to everyone and perhaps we were more vulnerable than the others. It was, in a sense, liberating.

We got massages and ate box lunches by the pool. We highlighted her hair and her youthful appearance began to return. We dressed for dinner and laid in matching canopied beds side by side at night and remembered the good memories. I told her funny stories and gave her a sense that life was good.

I couldn't lie to myself, though. She was failing. I could spot the beginning signs that her mind wasn't as clear as it had been. Small signs— not typical of PTSD but of the far more destructive dementia. She couldn't remember to put the toothpaste on the brush and instead squirted it in her mouth. She forgot to put out the lamp when we went to sleep and I caught her standing in the bathroom, a small yellow puddle around her feet and a horrified look on her face. She cried and said she'd forgotten why she went into the bathroom, and then it was too late.

It was heart breaking to see this. My mother, highly educated, and a member of one of the most famous political families in the United States had become confused, possibly demented. Far earlier than she should have. My mother, whose life had ostensibly ended almost forty years before when she married a monster. She'd been cheated in life. It broke my heart, but it was what it was.

I held her, told her I would take care of her and when she went to get her hair done at the salon, I closeted myself with her doctor and we discussed options. For the time being, she could care for herself, especially in an insulated environment like the hotel. But the time would come, and it wasn't far away, when she wouldn't be capable. The doctor felt it was less dementia and more PTSD, but I wasn't sure. It wasn't my specialty and I'd talk to others when I got back to Washington. For the time being, she was safe, and I could go back knowing that the inevitable would come one day and I'd have to be ready.

Our last lunch was in the tearoom. We laughed as we each had our third slice of the delicious cheesecake. I teased about ordering an entire cake to take with me and suddenly, she burst into tears.

"I don't want you to leave." Her blue eyes swam with tears. "I don't think I'll ever see you again."

I touched her hand. "I know and I don't want to leave. But Mom, this is the safest place for you right now."

Her eyes widened and I could have bitten the end of my tongue off.

"I thought you said he was really gone; that it wasn't him responsible for that awful attack."

What can I say?

"Mom, the Agency is making sure there's no one following his plans, picking up the vendetta. Just as soon as they're sure, I'll come get you myself and take you home. Why not come live with me in D.C.? We'll buy a house with plenty of room. We'll have a swimming pool and I'll hire someone to make cheesecakes like this for us."

She brightened at that. "You lie so well, my sweet. I thank you for being willing to do that. I know what you know and together we will get through this. That much I know."

I just smiled, teary-eyed with cheesecake stuck to the corner of my mouth. Melody reached to wipe it away and she put her fingertip into her own mouth. "Blood of my blood," she said. "Now, kiss me and go."

I did and even though I turned to wave a dozen times, I felt like I was leaving a dog at the pound to die. I hated the sensation, but the best thing I could do for her was to go back and make sure, with Jeff's help, that the Emir was truly gone forever. Only then could we rest in peace.

Chapter 19

"I missed you."

I turned in shock at the words that came from the toughest cookie in Walter Reed. She stood there in her navy blue skirt, white blouse with the round collar and her sensible shoes. She wore her string of pearls. Someone important must be around. She never wore pearls unless some uppity-up or a General was due.

"Frances?" I was surprised to see her. I suppose my voice gave me away.

My loyal assistant cracked a smile. "Good to hear at least you remember my name."

"Oh, now that's not fair. I've been…"

"No, no excuses." Her voice was brisk. "Well, you're back now. Let's get some work done. We'll try this again, shall we? Your patient files are on your desk and the first one is sitting half naked in Exam Room 4."

"Yes, ma'am. Who important is in house today?" I saluted her.

"That's better. What do you mean who important is in house today?"

I winked at her. "Someone is here. Someone important. I see you are wearing your pearls, and everyone knows you only wear jewelry when some high-up muckety- muck is on post."

Frances grinned and rolled her eyes. "You, you're the muckety-muck today."

I am sure my face was shocked. "What? You wore your pearls for me? Wow."

Frances didn't reply but left me alone in my office.

I smiled to myself and went over the first record, fighting for concentration. I'd rented a car to return from White Sulphur Springs and I admit to pulling over a couple times to rest. This recuperation business was serious and I needed to gain patience. But still, after a week of vacation, at a spa nonetheless, I was still under the weather.

I kept that in mind as I tended to the young woman in Exam Room 4. She was just back from the Middle East and although her face was tanned, she coughed continually, and I knew she'd been exposed to something toxic. I ordered tests and spent time with her. I knew how important it was for our soldiers to get attention. No civilian doctor could deal with the battle scars; few had the sympathy to even admit it and refer them. Her name was Janet and she was headed home to her two young children. Her husband had been busy playing both parenting roles and she missed all of them terribly. She needed my okay for her release.

Janet's lungs were scarred, and we discussed different things that had happened to her in battle. She'd been exposed to not only the environmental challenges, but gases and shrapnel from exploding devices. She was lucky to be alive. I looked at her determined face and knew she would need that strength years down the road when her body would begin to succumb to the effects of that exposure. Most likely she would develop breathing issues, if not worse. There was little I could do except evaluate, develop a plan for coping with the injuries, prescribe a few medicines and send her on home to her loving family. They were the best medicine available to her. That realization made me think about Melody again. God, how I'd hated leaving her.

Jeff and I hadn't had a chance to cross paths since I'd gotten back. He phoned to suggest we go out to dinner and I welcomed it.

We met at Tucker's, a family-owned restaurant that had a lovely garden with tables in back for eating al fresco. Jeff was waiting when I arrived and he stood, a bouquet of flowers in his hand. We'd parted a bit tense and it felt good to feel his loving kiss and feel his strong arms around me. Somehow, no matter how bad things were, he always seemed to make things better.

We ordered and after the drinks were served, he broached the topic we'd both been waiting for. "How was she?" he asked.

I grimaced and shrugged slightly. It's hard to tell what's due to her age and what's trauma. She has onset dementia, no question, but I didn't see any evidence of a psychosis. She's in a good place for now but I want to bring her closer, Jeff. I want her to live with us—well, at least with me if you're not of a like mind."

"Of course, she can live with us, but we'll need a bigger place."

I grinned. "That goes without saying. Three of us in the one bedroom is a bit much." I giggled at the thought. "I still have the insurance money from my house waiting in my account." I poked at the paper napkin with my fork, thoughtful. "Plus, Melody has her house we can put on the market."

"Let's start looking this week. I can leave the apartment anytime. Are you up for house hunting?"

I smiled at Jeff. I was so lucky to have him. "There's no one I'd rather house hunt with!"

Jeff picked up his wine glass and we toasted. I had a warm feeling in my stomach. After the toast, reality set in. "Well, what about Faisal?" I searched his eyes.

"You want to know?"

"Of course." I ignored the cramps in my stomach.

"Well, from all the evidence at the scene and the lab work from the victims and the bombs themselves, I'm sorry to say that it's either him or one of his trainees. The signs are unmistakable."

I flinched. I'd known it, but hearing Jeff say it somehow made it more powerful. Sighing, I asked. "What's the Agency's position?"

"They're operating under just that assumption. They're following up clues and whether it's him, or a protégé, either way we'll get him. I promise you."

"Jeff, let's be up front here. When it comes to the Emir, you can't promise anything. It's a matter of luck, because his planning is too thorough."

"Give us some credit, Sonia. He isn't the only one capable of long-term planning and tracking. We've caught our share of men just like him. It's a matter of time."

"Time... and bait, you mean. That's what Melody and I are, Jeff."

Our meal came. I pushed my plate away. I'd lost my appetite.

"Not hungry?"

"No. It's that visceral reaction to any thought of him. Gets me right in the guts."

"I can understand that. Would you like to leave?"

I looked down at my plate. "Would you mind terribly if we put this in a doggy bag and ate it back at the apartment?"

"No, not at all." Jeff signaled the waiter and gave instructions. An hour later we were home, sitting cross-legged on the bed with plates in our hands and watching the news. The last remnants of the explosion attack were still newsworthy, if for no better reason than to say they were still following up.

"People are spooked," Jeff explained.

"I imagine they are. I happen to know exactly how they feel." My stomach cramped again.

Jeff put his plate down on the nightstand and took the remote away from me, flipping off the news. "Look, Sonia. We need to talk."

I felt a thud in my stomach. This didn't sound very good.

"You know how I feel about you. You've known it for a long time. We ignored it as long as there was Paul..." he drifted off in the awkward moment. "Look, Sonia, I'm in love with you. Please, would you marry me? Let's live as man and wife, let me take care of you and find us a way out of this maze into some kind of a normal life. You've already retired and I'm ready any time. We can move out of D.C. Away from all this. Let's go to Virginia, buy a place and Melody can come live with us. We'll build her a mother-in-law apartment and hire help when she gets to be too much for you to take care of. You can meet ladies and go to lunch and I can play golf and come home to you every night. What do you say?"

My jaw was open as I listened. It was the last thing I'd expected him to say. I told him that. "Where did this come from?"

"I've asked you to marry me. You knew it would come eventually and if you want to wait a little longer, out of respect, well, I'm fine with that. But you and I, we're the same kind of people."

Once I found my voice, I said, "Let me think about it, would you? I love you, too. That's not it.

It's just that I didn't see this coming and I've been making my own plans. Just give me a week to think about it? After all, it would be a major change in my life."

Jeff leaned closer and wrapped his arms around me, plate of salad and all. "Of course. A week," he agreed. He took my salad, turned off the light on the nightstand and gave me more reasons to say yes for half the night.

Chapter 20

My day had gone well, and I'd finished at the hospital earlier than I'd anticipated. I took advantage of that time to go shopping for some new clothes. Agent Smith, a new one this time, was trailing behind and I could tell she had her eye on a few things and was probably miserable that she couldn't try something on. "It's okay, if you want to try something on. I'll stay close by," I told her.

She shook her head. "No, I really shouldn't. I'm on duty."

I stopped a moment to look at her and ask, "Just as a matter of curiosity, does the Agency ask you not to speak to your assignment, or to do something like maybe play gin rummy with me, if asked?"

Her bottom lip rolled out as she had a thoughtful frown. "No, I wouldn't think so. Just so we maintain watch, it's fine. I can't get drunk with you, of course. Why do you ask?" She gave me a strange look.

I shook my head. "No special reason. I just have more curiosity than any one person should, is all." I picked up a red sweater and pretended to consider it as I remembered the way Ester avoided having anything to do with me, using regulations as her excuse. I guess she just didn't like me, and that was basically okay with me. I didn't care for her either.

I'd been giving thought to Jeff's proposal. I loved him, and I think I secretly had for a very long time. He'd been my handler when I was on missions and my friend when I wasn't. That sort of relationship builds trust—it must in order to function. I'd known for some time that he was attracted to me and that he cared. He'd held back, respecting my commitment to Paul. His proposal had come very soon after losing Paul, and maybe that was one reason I asked him for some time to think about it. I had a suspicion that he felt he needed to make his feelings clear before I wandered off in some other direction. I had to admit I'd been scattered. My thoughts had circled around my health, Melody's situation and the questions about my father.

We finished up our shopping and headed back to the apartment and Agent Smith's shift change. I busied myself making a nice dinner and was surprised when Jeff came home early.

"Hello there," he greeted me, kissing me on the cheek.

"You're home early. That makes both of us. Thought I'd see if I could remember my recipe for lasagna. It's been so long since I've made it."

"Smells delicious. Have you got a minute? We need to talk."

179

I opened the oven door and slid in the baking dish, checking the temperature and wiping my hands on a towel. "Perfect timing. Want a drink?"

"Me? You go on ahead. I can't."

"Uh-oh. That sounds like something unexpected came up."

"I'm afraid so. Here, let's sit down. I'll have an iced tea, though, or lemonade. I am thirsty now that you bring it up."

I handed him a glass of tea and took my own over to sit on the sofa next to him. "Okay, so what's up?"

"I'm leaving later this evening on a mission."

"Oh. Can you tell me how long you'll be gone?"

"You know I can't, but let's just say I won't be home for dinner tomorrow night."

That was code to me that it was a long trip.

"Will you be visiting *family* while you're away?"

He knew I was asking whether he was going back to the Middle East, but we couldn't speak of it directly with another agent outside the door and who knew what other sort of monitoring equipment was in the apartment.

"Possibly." It was one word that spoke volumes.

I knew what was coming, so I took over the steering. "I know I said I would give you an answer in a week, Jeff. I'm not going anywhere and as much as I'd like to say *yes* right here and now, there are things that need to be sorted out first. Can we just postpone things for a bit?"

I could almost see the relief in his body language. That told me he might be gone quite a while and that part made me sad. He recognized that and once again, our bond strengthened because we had the ability to communicate almost subliminally. We always had. He nodded. "How long before that's out of the oven?"

"Give it an hour."

"Think I'll shower, and I have some packing to do."

We weren't even going to have the evening together. I stiffened a little at the thought of him leaving. Paul had left and look what happened. I didn't think I could go through it again. Instead, I smiled encouragingly, got up and gave him a brief kiss before heading back to the kitchen to butter some garlic bread. The afternoon and evening went by quickly, and before I knew it, he was gone.

It wasn't even eight o'clock yet, and he was gone. I went to bed; lonely, sad and very, very thoughtful. I knew the longer I put off marriage, the longer he'd be in the field. Yet, I needed his help there to resolve the matter about the Emir. Was I putting him in harm's way as my own sacrifice? I was very much afraid I was and that nagged at me all night.

Chapter 21

My driver was a new girl that next morning. She barely looked old enough to drive, but perhaps it was me who was getting older. It felt like so much of my life was already a missed opportunity.

"Dr. Amon," the girl said, her eyes darting to the rearview mirror, "I'd just like to say it's a pleasure to spend time with you. I've heard so many wonderful things about you."

I smiled back. It always felt good to have a pat on the back. "Are you allowed to tell me your first name?"

"Sure. I'm Patsy—well, it's Patricia, but my friends call me Patsy."

"Well, Patsy, you are a welcomed addition to the group who have been looking out for me. It's nice to have someone to talk to."

"Oh? Am I not supposed to?"

"Of course, you may. It's just been that not all the agents have been as willing or want to. Never mind. So, where are you from, Patsy?" I admitted to myself I was asking that on purpose; it was a test.

"Tennessee. Sevierville, Tennessee. Same place as Dolly Parton. We can't help but be friendly, coming from there, you know."

"Really?" I was impressed. I admired Dolly Parton. "She's a very talented lady, and a good businesswoman, too, from what I understand."

"She sure is. She's got a big heart, and I don't mean that in the slimy way. Did you know she gives tons of money for books so the mountain kids will have a good education? I guess you could say she comes just about as close to being a queen for those parts as anybody could. We just love her."

I thought Dolly would be a pretty good Queen and said so. I adored Patsy and her enthusiasm, and it was contagious. We chatted all the way into Walter Reed and the time passed in seconds. When she opened the door for me, I squeezed her arm. "I like you and appreciate the visit. Let's see if we can't get you assigned to me more often, shall we?"

"Yes, ma'am, Dr. Amon. I'd just love that." She wore a grin as big as a sunny sky.

Frances met me with a cup of coffee and a Danish. "You know where you'll find your records for the day," she said. I noticed she looked pale.

"Frances, are you okay? You're looking peaked."

"Just a bug. I'll be fine." Her voice was crisp, but her eyes were tired and fatigue showed on her face.

"What are your symptoms?" I set down the coffee. I'd never known her to be sick as long as she'd worked with me and if I believed the rumors,

Frances hadn't been sick or missed a day of work in thirty years. "Follow me."

For once she did as she was told and that, in of itself, told me she wasn't feeling well. Frances *always* argued, if only to have the last word.

I examined her. The heart rhythm was irregular, and she had a flushed face. "How long have you felt this way?"

"Two days, ma'am. Haven't been able to keep anything down."

I called for a phlebotomist and ordered a complete blood panel. "I'm sending you home, my driver will take you. Unless you think you'd rather be admitted?"

"No. Home will be fine, ma'am." Her face paled and she looked away from me.

I studied her. She was being highly formal; so unlike the craggy matron who kept my life in order. In a way, that frightened me. I went into the hallway and called out, "Agent Smith?"

Patsy was just around the corner and popped her head, a Danish in her hand. "Ma'am?"

"I want you to drive Captain Haran home immediately. She's not feeling well."

Patsy's mouth dropped open. "Ma'am, I'm sorry, but I'm not allowed. I'm to remain with you."

"Patsy, I don't have time to argue. I'll take responsibility. Get the car."

"Yes, ma'am," she answered, dumping her Danish in a nearby trash. "Right away, Ma'am." I saw her pull out her cell as she hurried down the hallway. I knew she was reporting the change in plans to her superiors.

I went back to Frances who was bent over a basin. I wondered whether she had the same virus I'd had. I wrapped her in a blanket and summoned an orderly to take her down to the entrance in a wheelchair. "Don't worry. I will stay in touch. It's probably what I had, and it's icky, but it goes away."

She nodded and as I watched, my second mother was wheeled down the hallway and I suddenly felt even more alone, if that was possible. I considered how sick the virus had made me, and Frances was much older. I was genuinely worried.

As luck had it, there were only two more patients on the blotter for the day, so as soon as they were done, I headed for some lunch and went back to my office to eat at my desk. I had a handful of medical publications I kept up with, and I read through those quickly for anything that was relevant.

The sense of loneliness drove me into a dark place, and I searched for my father's name. His face came up on the first screen and I found myself staring into my own eyes. My reaction was a tensing of my stomach muscles and a burgeoning sense of panic. I told myself I was safe; that he was probably dead and at the very least, nowhere near me.

I knew if I was ever going to overcome my visceral reaction to him, it was going to take repeated efforts at desensitization. I forced myself to look at his picture, to think of him as a man who was my father and not the man who was hunted for killing thousands. It hurt, but I forced myself to stay with it.

It wasn't just one website. There were news reports, sites that supported him which were filled with radicals against everything in general – certainly in the Western World and then there were Syrian sites where he was praised, honored and revered written in Arabic.

One site was biographical, and I was surprised to see pictures of myself when I was a child; even one with Melody.

That's when I saw the photo that changed everything—everything in life that mattered to me and quite possibly my life itself.

The photo was probably ten years-old and showed Faisal sitting in a casual setting, most likely where he was living at the time. I even recognized the two men seated nearby. The men were eating as a woman served them. One very young woman kneeled next to my father, her face turned up to his and her hand lovingly on his cheek.

It was Ester. *Oh my God. It was Ester.* My heart stopped beating. I could hardly breathe!

I screamed—literally screamed aloud as the ramifications punched their way into my consciousness. My father was an only child. A female, that young and that close to him could only mean one thing.

Ester was my half-sister; his daughter!

And she hated me. Now I understood.

Chapter 22

Hell was my reality. Panic consumed me. With Frances gone, I was mentally flailing, a maelstrom of indecision and fear taking over. Terror chilled my blood. I knew I was having an anxiety attack but the nature of such an event precludes your having the logic to externally recognize that fact.

I grabbed for my phone when two soldiers came running in, having heard me scream.

"Get Jeff! You have to get to Jeff!" I babbled. I needed to pull myself together. To be coherent. I didn't need Dr. Fish Eyes in my life again.

"Get a chair and whoever's on duty," one said to the other and he nodded and disappeared. I was shaking, the soldier with me kept telling me to breathe. I could only imagine the alarm that was shooting around the hospital halls about me.

Naturally, they called Fish Eyes, who promptly pulled a syringe and stabbed me in the arm. "She's having a PTSD episode," he diagnosed on the spot to the waiting soldiers. "I'll take her from here." They saluted and left. Milliken pushed me down the hallway toward the elevators. I was having trouble forming my words and I felt so weary I could barely keep my eyes open.

The doors swished open and there stood Agent Smith, aka Patsy.

"Patsy!" I blurted, although to my ears it sounded like gibberish. "Help me!"

Patsy put an arm out to stop Milliken from pushing me into the elevator. I heard him speak behind me. "Security. Elevator 3-B."

"Step aside," Milliken ordered. "She is a patient and needs immediate treatment."

"Nooo..." I cried out, begging Patsy with my eyes to help me. I tried to reach out but looked down to see that I'd been cuffed to the chair.

I heard scuffling behind me. "Stand down, Agent!" shouted a new male voice.

Patsy gave me a look of desperation and pity. I couldn't say anything because I didn't know who could be trusted. "Get to Jeff! Emergency!" I cried out to her.

I never saw anything as welcome as when she smiled, gave me a thumbs up and a smile. "Consider it done."

I felt so, so sleepy...Fish Eyes had tried to put me out. I tried to fight it but it was hard, almost impossible.

There was motion and the thump-thump sound of tires as they passed over the cracks of an older concrete road. I kept my eyes closed and listened.

"Did you search her?" an accented voice asked.

"She's clean. I took care of it." The voice that answered was familiar. In my stupor it took a few seconds but then I recognized it. Milliken! Milliken was in the car. *Where were they taking me?* Ice-cold fear clogged my blood vessels. I could hardly breathe.

"She jerked. I think she's waking up."

"Give her more." The voice sounded angry, irritated.

I felt the pinch and then the heaviness returned.

This time, as the world began to fade in, I knew to stay motionless. There didn't seem to be anyone close by; no sense of energy, no breathing or body heat. Maintaining my frozen position for some minutes, I finally deduced that I was, indeed alone. I cracked first one eye, only as far as the length of my eyelash, and then only for a second.

The room was utilitarian. Concrete block walls and a cement floor. I was lying on a bed; more to the point, I was handcuffed to it. I didn't dare move my hands in case the cuffs made a metallic sound that would attract undesirable attention. My eyes combed my surroundings. It appeared as though I was in some old military quarters. The door was solid, no window and only a lock in the handle from the inside. I had no idea if it was locked from the outside as well.

It was quiet; so quiet that I couldn't hear ambient noises at all. No birds, wind, voices— nothing, other than a faint buzz. The only other sound was that of my own breathing and at that moment, it was coming in rapid spurts from fear.

There was an Army green woolen blanket spread over me, but no sheets. The bed was made of metal with a thin blue-tick mattress. Things smelled stuffy, as though they needed a good airing out. I also caught a whiff of mold every now and then. At that moment, there was a click, after which I felt air moving in through a register mounted in the wall, a tiny black ribbon elevated by its strength.

Very, very slowly, I pushed downward with my leg. It seemed unfettered and I rejoiced that I would be able to move freely. In thinking about it, I doubted anyone would administer further drugs as it seemed we'd arrived at the destination and I was properly confined. The question was, where was I? I searched my mind for possibilities.

The only source of light was a single, long fluorescent bulb mounted in a bracket centered on the room's ceiling. It was flickering slightly as they often do when they're about to burn out. That's where the buzzing came from. Even though the flicker was annoying, I hoped it would continue to live, as would I.

I closed my eyes again, certain that if anything in the room was to change, I would hear it. I wanted to think without distraction; to put together the facts so I'd be prepared. For what, I had no clue, but at least it felt as though I was doing something useful—coming up with a plan.

Panic flowed through me like hot lava. I remembered back to gather my facts. Ester was his offspring; there was no doubt about it. I realized why her eyes looked so familiar to me. They weren't that dissimilar from my own. I don't know why anyone close to me hadn't picked up on that, but then we'd never stood side by side as far as I could recall. What was she doing working for the Agency? I was certain they had no idea of her past. They vetted everyone. How had she gotten past their checks? She obviously had infiltrated the Agency barriers. If anyone could do it, it was my father. His evil was only surpassed by his intelligence and it was likely that he'd bribed American ex-agents to give him insider information. The question was, did this mean the Emir was dead, or alive?

Melody! She was down at the resort, unaware of the danger. I knew without question that Ester's mission was to kill me, and my mother. The advantage I had was that I knew that and could avoid her. My mother was a sitting duck. Chills raced up my body. I tried to remember the last time I'd seen Ester. It was the evening when I'd been lonely. I'd asked her to visit with me and she'd behaved strangely. She'd been rude and given me short, impolite, almost boorish answers.

It was likely she went back to her handler, perhaps it was my father himself, and reported that she was about to be given up — that she has blown her cover. There was only as far she could go without revealing herself. I'd almost caught her; if I'd paid attention would have realized this. *I should have caught her.* Rage raced through my body. I chastised myself for not seeing all of it.

Jeff! He'd had the enemy in his midst and had no clue, just as I'd had no clue. There was no telling how much valuable information she'd passed along; how many lives she'd been responsible for. I thought of the bombing of the mosque. I wondered if she'd masterminded part of that.

Even Milliken was part of the Emir's intelligence community. He was a man of low character; the type who would undoubtedly fold at the sight of money. He'd never amount to anything in his career on his own, so why not go to the highest bidder? Was he working for one of my father's soldiers; promised riches or a position in the high command in Syria? In the U.S. he was a physician, an individual that satisfied a slot in staffing. He was in a veteran's medical care center where he held considerable power. His practice required every soldier substantiate his own illness and connect it to an event that could have caused it. Milliken was dirty.

My mind continued to wonder. Then there was Frances; the stalwart mothering friend who had never been sick in her life. Was there more to this than the virus? Was this biological sabotage? The coincidence between her symptoms and my own were worth investigation at the very least.

For every conjecture, there was a handful of evidence that could support the result. How many of us were in danger? How many other betrayals were not yet uncovered? What was the ultimate plan and most of all, how could I stop it all in time?

Jeff! I needed Jeff. He always waited on the outside of my ring of familial madness, holding one hand out to me so I could jump out at will and return to normalcy. When I worked with the Agency, it was always a Ferris wheel. Round and round with only that solitary point at the bottom when I could jump out or be carried upward again where there was no footing, nothing to hold onto that stayed still. I felt dizzy, no doubt from whatever medicine Milliken had been giving me. For now, all I could do was to sleep. I wished my hands were free, although they'd serve no additional purpose. Except, perhaps, I would feel less helpless; although that seemed to be what I was destined to feel—helpless.

Somewhere, a key jiggled, metal scraped against concrete and I came awake. My eyes flew open; too late I remembered to pretend sleep.

"You're awake after all," came the voice I'd come to hate almost as much as my father's. It was Milliken.

"Where am I?"

He laughed, and it was a wicked sound; perhaps, only to me, though. "I'll tell you this much. No one will hear you scream."

The man was vile. A chill ran downward from my shoulders to my gut. "Will I be screaming?" I asked in the most matter-of-fact way I could manage.

"Probably."

After a few moments, I summoned the courage to be defiant. "What do you want?"

"You forget how this works, Dr. Amon." He laughed again; that sound of dominance when your victim is at your mercy. "I ask the questions and *you* give the answers. Remember?"

"Very well. Unfasten my hands. If no one can hear me scream, you shouldn't be concerned."

"Now, that's more like it," he sniggered. "But no, that's not permitted. You'll have to make do." He reached toward me and set a bedpan on the bed next to me. "You should be needing that by now." He nodded toward the metal pan. "Go ahead. Your chains are long enough to accommodate that."

"Get me something to drink. I want water. My throat feels like cardboard."

"Of course, princess," he answered in a mocking voice. "That would be the antihistamine I added to the benzodiazepine. But then, you know all about that, don't you? I'll be right back."

I watched his retreating back. I loathed the man! Never again would anyone persuade me to ignore my butt instincts. He opened the door and it scraped as it closed behind him. He wasn't worried about my escaping because I was chained to the bed. I did need to use the bedpan and took advantage of his absence to do it. It helped snap my brain back to a sense of control. This gave me the presence of mind to plan an escape.

The door opened and Milliken entered, a plastic tray with plate and utensils—all made of flimsy plastic or Styrofoam. Was he afraid I'd hurt myself, or him? I knew which.

"Are you even a doctor?" I asked in a conversational tone, intent on keeping a dialogue going so I could obtain as much information as he was willing to divulge.

"I was, at one time," he admitted. "One little slip in judgment and I lost my practice."

"How did you get in Walter Reed?"

He laughed with gusto. "The government sometimes overlooks things in their haste." He grinned at me, evil flooded his face. "And then, there's always the possibility of false documents."

I found his statement interesting. "You're saying they didn't vet you thoroughly?"

"I'm saying they needed someone to handle post battle traumas. A man of my credentials could make six to eight times what they pay me in his own practice."

Unfortunately, I knew he was speaking the truth. "So, my father's organization made you that offer you couldn't refuse," I summarized for him. I was drawing upon his vanity; his sense of self-worth had been damaged by whatever incident ended his legitimate practice. He felt the need to justify and re-establish his value.

"Something like that." He winked at me and grinned. Chill bumps worked their way up my spine.

Aha. He's working for Faisal! I wondered if he was good enough at his job to understand the ramifications of terror his careless talk had caused.

"I want to see him." It was a bold demand, but it would tell me so much.

"I'm sure you do. That, however, won't be possible."

"Why not?" I shot back.

"Eat while you can. I'm growing weary with this game you're playing and I'm about to leave. The food goes with me." Maybe he wasn't as obtuse as I'd hoped. I picked up the food and sniffed it.

He laughed. "You think you can smell if it's drugged? You should know better than that, Dr. Amon. After all, you haven't up to now."

What did that mean? Had I been given drugs without my knowing it? The bug! Like a belated thunder, I quivered as I realized what he was saying. Of course! It wasn't a bug. I was being slowly, systematically poisoned. I threw the food down without taking a bite.

"Oh, sweet Dr. Amon. There would be little point in adding anything to your food now. After all, we have you where we want you. There's no escape. You're buried alive. I don't want to clean up a mess. The food is safe. Eat it and perhaps you'll stay alive long enough to at least plan an escape."

I was fighting the panic that flooded downward from my brain. *How could he destroy my confidence with a few words?* That was it! He was feeding on my insecurities. He was right, of course. Whatever they'd been giving me had made me vomit and have diarrhea. They wouldn't want that mess. I took the food from the tray, eating it and downing the glass of water with defiance.

He chuckled. "I thought you'd see the sense of it."

"When are you going to kill me?" I boldly demanded to know.

He stretched his arms over his head with a yawn. "Tsk, tsk, tsk..." he yawned as he whispered. "That part will be left to someone else. My job here is almost done. Will you miss me?"

That left me with a decision. If I said I wouldn't, it would undermine his maniacal sense of self-worth and he could grow angry—violent even. If I flattered him, he could see through it and that might be an even bigger insult. He wasn't stupid. I chose the safer path. "What do you think?" Always answer the unanswerable with another question.

He laughed, standing and coming close to gather my utensils. "Enjoy your evening, Dr. Amon. Someone will bring a clean bedpan." He jerked at the handle on the door and holding it open with his shoulder, and then his hip, he left me, eating like a starving animal with my hands.

When silence regained the room, I set what I hadn't eaten at the furthest corner of my mattress, next to where my head would lie. I would save it. It was strategic to save whatever you had when escape was the objective. You never knew how you might use it.

It did feel better to drink the water and put something in my stomach, though. I marveled at the strength of food. When I'd awakened, my stomach was upset with fear. Now, I knew more — even if it wasn't good news. Now I could channel my panic into determination. Confidence makes a much better cellmate.

Settling back into a prone position, I tallied the information I'd garnered from our conversation. Without assumptions, I tried to be absolutely impartial. First, there was the fact that Fish Eyes wasn't at the bottom of this incarceration. He was working for someone else. He'd mentioned that someone would bring a clean bedpan. That told me he wasn't alone as my sole captor. Someone else, most likely someone in an inferior position would be doing that. I had to reason that the person was female. Someone who was used to taking orders and carrying them out without question. Someone who knew nothing. They couldn't trust anyone with valuable knowledge to come in my cell. Fish Eyes was a trained doctor; capable of recognizing my masked attempts at gaining information. Even his knowledge was limited. That was proven by the fact that I'd given him ample opportunity to brag, and he had, up to a point. At that point, he would be claiming something untrue.

Was our conversation being monitored? That was entirely possible. I looked slowly around the room, trying to pick out any irregularity in the room's construction. Was there a wire with a tiny microphone? Perhaps a speaker designed to look like an electrical socket? An air vent? Yes! There was a vent.

I took a deep breath. Other than the door itself, the vent was the most likely source of monitoring. It could accommodate a speaker and a camera without problem. I tried not to stare at it. I lay at an angle on the mattress, my hand over my forehead and eyes, as though I was rubbing them in worried thinking. I peeked through my fingers; glancing at the vent, gauging its height from the floor and assessing if any part of the room might be safe from its position. Just to make things look normal, I flung myself on my side, away from the vent with an exasperated sigh. It wasn't that far from the truth, especially when the cuffs cut me short like a dog pulling at her leash.

The drugs were wearing off. I could feel my extremities and now that I was plotting, my panic was receding.

Who was holding me and what did they want?

The second part of that question was more obvious. They wanted me dead. The first part was trickier. It had to lead back to my father; I hadn't antagonized anyone else in my life to the point they'd want to kill me. If it wasn't him, it was someone close to him; someone who understood his tactics. Ester? I doubted it. She could have killed me many times over as I slept.

Ester had been behind the illness. She had access, knowledge and an alibi. I recalled my symptoms; typical of several methods but my bet was on arsenic. Frances had almost the identical symptoms and I'd seen those before. I bet her test results came back showing that. Were they after her, too? Or had she simply innocently eaten or drank something intended for me?

So many questions. So many possibilities. Only one solution. I had to get out of wherever I was. I had to find a way to get to Melody. She didn't know they were after her. I'd done her the questionable favor by taking her off high alert.

There was a greater danger at hand, however. The Agency had a mole. It had been infiltrated and the clock was ticking until their plan would be executed. Hell only knew how many lives that may involve.

I felt like the bomb that was ticking. I was the eventuality, and someone had set the timer.

Closing my eyes, I'd had enough rest that I could feign sleep for quite some time. My watch paid off when the door opened again, and someone came in to set the promised bed pan on my mattress. I peeked and saw it was a woman, wearing a jilbab. She was precisely what I suspected. She turned on slippered feet and left. I said nothing. Time was on my side—at least for the moment.

I found a comfortable position and went back to sleep. I would need my wits about me if I was to escape wherever I was.

Chapter 23

The sound of a key in the lock and then the scraping of the door awakened me. I'd had trouble sleeping; a combination of having rested while being drugged and the infernal buzz and blinking of the bright light overhead. I could see how that could comprise torture all by itself.

The woman returned, this time to bring a tray and wait as I used the bedpan. She removed it without a word and left me to eat and think. The meal was quite tasty, and the Styrofoam had been replaced by a plastic container with sections, much as you'd find at a salad bar to go at the grocery. One section held scrambled eggs, another fried potatoes with onion, the third section held a small biscuit and the fourth held a pat of butter and a commercial foil tub of strawberry jam. There was an accompanying white linen napkin that clothed plastic eating utensils. Coffee in a plastic mug with a lid and a small restaurant-supply container of orange juice completed the meal.

I took my time eating, enjoying the flavor and knowing it might be the only pleasure I'd have during the day—perhaps it was even my last meal. I had no way of knowing. I set aside, as thoroughly as I could, the worries that floated around my head. My mother, Jeff, Frances, the people who would be harmed—it was too much. All I could do was pray that Patsy had interpreted my situation and found a way to alert Jeff. It was unlikely as I knew from our joint missions that the first three to four days were always intense. That's when you were first dropped into the point of action and you worked quickly at your mission, hoping you wouldn't be discovered. I had no idea, naturally, what Jeff's assignment entailed, but I knew he would be the least accessible early on.

The second and perhaps only other possible savior was Frances. If she'd been poisoned by accident, by removing her from the hospital she was likely separated from the contaminated food or drink. At home she would be able to recover fairly quickly. I knew her stubborn nature. She'd be back at work and demanding to know where I was. She wouldn't be put off. She'd get to the bottom of things and she carried some weight around the place. Plus, she, of all people, could get to Jeff.

My prayer was that they weren't given the story that Milliken was trying to circulate; that I was merely exhibiting the symptoms of PTSD. Yet, they'd have to produce me, somehow. Jeff wouldn't take anyone's word for where I was. My guess was that Milliken would suggest that he'd placed me in a mental institution for my own safety and the institution's policy was no visitors for the first 72 hours. That would give my captors the window of time they needed for whatever they had planned for me.

Melody – my sweet mother who was living in her own delirium. She was being used as a control to keep me cooperating. I just wished I knew their objective.

I finished the meal and dabbed at my mouth with the napkin. Something caught my eye. I was careful not to react. I held it in my hand as if it was a security blanket, dabbing at my dry eyes as though I was crying. I laid back down and turned onto my hip again, putting my back to the vent. Examining the napkin furtively, I found what had caught my eye. It was the faintest watermark woven into the fabric. It was two letters: G and H.

Folding the fabric over my hand, I rubbed my wrists with it where the cuffs had chaffed, and the skin was red and nearly bleeding. I pretended to fall asleep, still holding onto it.

Sure enough, the woman appeared shortly thereafter and took the tray. She obviously overlooked the napkin I clutched against my chest in my hand. That told me two things. I was clearly being monitored because she knew when to return, and secondly, I was being held somewhere nice enough to warrant restaurant supply packaging and initialed linen napkins.

The answer came at me like an arrow shot from Heaven. Greenbriar Hotel! I was being held at the same location where Melody was staying! Of course. It all made sense. My room was one of the many bunker bedrooms built to house all of

Congress in case of a nuclear attack. I knew from researching it when Melody was being taken there, that the quarters I occupied were part of a mammoth underground bunker. While the leaked reports noted different depths and sizes, the roof of my building was said to be at least twenty feet below ground but built 720 feet into the hillside. It was built of feet-thick concrete, wire mesh and had a separate ventilation system from the hotel. It could not only bring in fresh air but could filter out radiation. It would be easy to put a camera into that shaft.

I thanked God for my medical training and my Army experience. It had taught me to watch for subtle details and use deductive thinking to solve medical mysteries. In this case, it was going to save my life. I was sure of it. Not only did I know where I was, I now knew roughly how the building was designed. What was more, I had a better idea of how to get out and Melody would be close by.

The ideas were like a dam about to burst in my mind. Each thought had ramifications; each concept its inherent set of dangers. I only had what was available to me within the room. For the moment, anything new came in and out with the dark-eyed woman wearing a jilbab. She brought my meals and so far, there had been a napkin on the tray. She'd opened my door with a key from the outside. Was it possible she also carried the key to my cuffs? It would be the logical thing to do. A plan began to take form for me. The problem was the timing. The longer I waited, the more informed I'd be on their routine. At the same time, if I waited too long, they could carry out whatever plans they had and it would be too late for me to do anything at all. One thing remained certain. If I did nothing, the worst of all scenarios would be carried out. That was unthinkable.

Chapter 24

I had taken after my father's side when it came to my height. I stood five feet, ten inches in my bare feet and while some people may consider that graceful and a model's build, I found myself looking down on balding heads much of the time. I was prepared.

Praying that no one was constantly watching me on a monitor, I picked up the wool blanket from the bunk and covered myself with it. Moving as quickly as I could, after wrapping my hand with the napkins I'd kept, I began jumping on the bed until I could reach and break the neon light overhead. The room was dark, but I'd memorized my position ahead of time. I threw off the blanket, now embedded with shards of glass, and rocked the bed hard away from the camera until it tipped on its side. I lay on the concrete, shaking but determined. It had the desired effect.

Within seconds I heard the key in the lock and the door scraped open. The woman in the jilbab flipped on a flashlight and pushed aside debris looking for me. When she rounded the foot of my bed, I lifted my arms as if to hug her but instead the chains of my cuffs formed a sort of noose. I pulled back tightly, the chain links choking her. She struggled, but I was the stronger of we two, and she eventually passed out. Just as I'd hoped, I could still feel a pulse, but she was unconscious.

As quickly as I could, I grabbed her flashlight and flipped it off. Again just as I'd hoped, one of the two keys dangling from the chain about her neck fit my cuffs and I wasted no time pulling them off and securing her to the bed.

I pulled at her jilbab, sliding it off her inert body and smoothly putting it on myself. I'd had practice but never dreamed I would use it to survive. With the head-dress carefully draped over most of my face, I flipped the flashlight back on and walked across the room, looked upward to the vent so only my dark eyes, a hereditary gift from the Emir, were visible. In quick Farsi, I said, "Do not be alarmed. I have it under control." For once, I was thankful for my Middle-Eastern looks.

I opened the door to the cell and locked it behind myself. Inhaling deeply, I knew I'd only accomplished half my goal. I was still a prisoner in a building buried deeper than a casket and had to find my way out. Luckily, the U.S. government was well-prepared and had mounted at intervals down the hallway, a floor plan diagram that clearly labeled where I was standing and how to get to the exit. It took only moments to get my bearings and determine where the command center, and likely my kidnappers, were positioned.

I heard footsteps coming my way and leaned over, covering myself with a huddled stature, as was expected of a Syrian woman. Hugging the wall as I walked, two men of Middle-Eastern origin passed me without a second glance. That told me there were women living on the compound.

My immediate goal was to get out of the building and find my mother, but I couldn't relieve myself of the responsibility I had to find out who else was in danger. It was no small operation and that told me the stakes were enormous. I recognized my father's hand in it. Who else would be cunning enough to take a U.S. government command center over and use it for the destruction I knew he most likely had planned? Who else, what other merciless killer would actually break in and commandeer the former underground White House? Not to mention how he'd managed to take over the huge facility.

I continued to hug the wall until I came to a crossroads in what appeared to be a highway of corridors. Another map was posted on the wall and I used my fingertip to plot the route and distance from where I stood to the command center, located appropriately in the middle of the diagram. It looked to be about fifty yards from where I was standing. To my right, about the same distance away, was one of four entrances. The facility had been closed for more than two decades, but much of it was as it had been when it was built in 1955.

The question was, what was he planning to do with it and did anyone else know? Was I the only person in the free world who knew that something cataclysmic, perhaps even bigger than 9/11 was in the planning stages? *This was my nightmare.* The fact that I'd been brought here, at this point, told me the show was about to begin.

I knew in my heart; I wasn't there to be kept safe. I had been brought there to watch my father's victory.

Chapter 25

If Faisal had done one thing for me as a child, it was to raise me to be selfless. Of course, in his estimation it was more like—worthless. I was a female child who should have been a male. A male he could have brought up at his knee, instructing him like a clone who would carry on his essence of violence and horror when his own body withered and finally collapsed.

As it was, being selfless meant that you would sacrifice for the greater good, and for that reason, I turned left.

As I did, a thought occurred to me that left me breathless and I stumbled briefly under its weight. *What if my father had sired a son with the same woman who had given him Ester? Could there be a second Faisal out there, wanting to kill me, the first-born?* The mere thought of that possibility took me to my knees. *A brother. Another generation of murder. Oh, my God!* For several moments I thought I'd pass out.

I went in search of the command center for any clues that would tell me what was planned. I'd had Agency training, but there had always been an advance team that gave me instructions and planned for eventualities. I had none of that now. I didn't even have Jeff to guide me from a distance.

Following the map, my destination was straight ahead. Men came and went more often the closer I got. None confronted me. I guessed that any women in the bunker had undergone personal vetting by whomever was in charge, so there were no boundaries or areas they were denied. Indeed, some of the best scientists and mathematicians in Syria were women. That would work in my favor. I knew I had a limited amount of time, though. The woman back in my cell would be stirring and shouting for help. I might have only minutes and could lose my chance to escape by a useless endeavor to stop what was going on.

Ahead I saw a series of half windows and on the inside, men were moving about, as were a very few women. There were banks of screens with people sitting at consoles. I noticed in a corner there was a stockpile of old computer monitors. Undoubtedly, they were ancient technology and had been replaced by the flat monitors I could see now. People were moving about, and I'd look out of place if I simply stood and stared. I had no choice. I had to attempt to go inside.

I pulled at the door and while the guard next to the door looked at me, he didn't seem to find any reason to stop me. I spotted an open chair and boldly crossed the room and sat there. I had a bank of monitors over my head and I quickly scanned them, trying to figure out what each represented. There were maps with blinking lights and a legend that indicated yellow meant "In Position", red meant "Armed and Ready" and green meant "Launched." Luckily for me, I could read the language, or it would have been a giant puzzle I could have only guessed at. Another monitor appeared to be tracking the weather. It showed much the same map as The Weather Channel except that this map charted wind flow patterns. A third monitor showed graphic circles around each of the blinking lights from the other monitor. As I translated the legend, I froze.

This monitor, larger than the others, predicted population decimation. The lights centered on high population areas along the east coast including New York City, Boston, Baltimore and Washington, D.C. The very seat in which I sat was included in the danger areas. Suddenly I realized what was going on.

These weren't bomb sites; not simple targets where unwilling suicide bombers would detonate themselves and take out maybe twenty people around them. No, indeed. This was a widespread area around each target, larger than a bomb. I swallowed hard.

They were planning to release biologicals along the east coast of the U.S. From New York City, through the nation's capital and right up to the doorstep of the bunker where I was sitting. The bunker, of course, was invulnerable—having been built to withstand nuclear fallout. *Oh my God. I was dizzy with knowledge and sick at the thought*

*of what would soon happen. A biological weapons
attack. From the underground White House. What
a feat for my bastard father.*

I gripped the counter and tried to look as
though I belonged there as panic overcame me. I
was consumed, almost powerless as I looked
around. One other monitor was a closed-circuit
camera and showed a hanger filled with odd-
looking, windowless small planes. Drones! They
planned to deliver the biologicals via drones. I
knew the Greenbriar had its own airstrip and due
to the altitude, and the frequency with which
private aircraft brought well-known guests, air
traffic controllers would give enormous latitude to
the resort air activity. They would literally green-
light their own demise! My heart raced in my
chest as I contemplated the eventualities. It was
horrific. I ignored the pain in my chest.

I had to leave. I couldn't believe I'd gone
undiscovered as long as I had. I picked up a folder
of papers and headed to the door. The guard held
out his weapon and blocked my exit.

I froze, my overtaxed heart pumped fear
through me. Looking straight ahead, I waited.
With the tip of his weapon, he prodded my long
over-jacket, the jilbab. I refused to flinch.
Eventually, he held out his hand for the folder.
There was no choice but to hand it over. He opened
it, quickly leafed through the sheets and then
handed it back. He tapped a button and the

automatic doors hissed as they opened. He motioned with his weapon that I was free to go.

This time I didn't hesitate. I walked slowly, but firmly against the wall, this time continuing straight ahead when I came to the intersection. The corridor was straight, lined by rooms with open doors that revealed bunk beds and living quarters. To my right I saw medical equipment, antiquated but unused. Eventually, ahead was a windowless green door, a heavy bar locked into position. I slowed and at the last minute, saw a button and a lever, which I pushed. The door swung open and I looked out into the West Virginia night. I was free!

Chapter 26

The portico outside the hotel was brightly lit.
I prayed that Melody was still there and that they
hadn't moved her inside the bunker. I ditched the
jilbab beneath a bush and walked confidently into
the hotel and up to the desk. I asked for my mother
by name and was directed to wait in the lobby and
they would notify her I was there.

I could barely sit because I was so nervous.
Potted palms and a string quartet did nothing to
calm me. The entire scene seemed surreal, as
though I was watching it through a thick sheet of
glass. I knew that was panic. I began deep
breathing, exhaling slowly over a count of eight.

A movement caught my eye as elevator doors
slid open and there she was, looking around in
confusion. Not wasting a second, I strode toward
her and linked my arm in hers. I kissed her cheek.
"Just follow my lead," I whispered in her ear and
headed for the entrance doors, smiling and
pointing out paintings and glassed exhibit cases as
we casually strolled out the door and down the
sidewalk. I pretended we were headed toward the
guest cabins that lined the pool and riding arena.
I spoke softly, staying as calm as I could while still
trying to hurry her along.

"I don't understand, darling. Where are we going? It's nighttime, you know. I was just putting on my gown to go to bed."

I hugged her shoulders. "Mom, I know. Don't be alarmed, but we're in trouble and we must disappear until I can get help. Remember how we did it before? Years ago? Remember how we clung together and tried to look normal, but we were running away?"

"Yes, I think I do." She hesitated. Her faced looked confused.

"I don't want to make him mad, Sonia. You know what he does to me when he's angry." My mother lived every single day with the tortuous nightmare of my father. No one deserved that.

"That's not going to happen, Mom." My voice was quiet and steady. "This is different. We just need to get help. I'm not sure how. I don't know anyone here and the hotel is the only establishment here on the mountain. No houses. I don't know who's in on it, so I don't know who to trust."

"Would this help?" Melody asked, holding out her cell phone.

"Mom! My God, you're wonderful!" I kissed her on the cheek and hugged her. Checking the phone, it was fully charged and had three bars. I felt on top of the world. Now came the question. *Who to call?* There was only one number I knew would be answered without question.

I called the main line for Walter Reed.

"Dr. Amon's office, please," I asked, praying that Frances had somehow managed to get in. It was nighttime, but her number was forwarded to her home if she didn't answer it.

"Hello?" It was Frances, but her voice was weak and I hated myself for having to disturb her. I knew how horrible I'd felt.

"Frances! It's me, Sonia. Can you talk? Is someone there with you?"

"Only my sister, Beatrice."

Sister? All this time and I didn't know that Frances had a sister? "Frances, I need you and this is Code Red. We can't talk on this phone, it's not secure. Be careful what you say. Listen carefully. You must reach him—the man who always looks after me."

"Yes, I understand." Her voice was stronger. The iron maiden was kicking in, despite her misery.

"Tell him code red. Do you understand? Code Red. Melody's place, Code Red. Can you remember that?" I visualized her pale face and iron-grey hair.

"I might be sick, but I'm not an idiot. I've got that. It might take some time, he..."

"Yes, yes, I know. But there's no other choice. Do it, Frances. My life and maybe even yours depends on it. Oh, and Frances. Do not eat anything or drink anything that isn't freshly brought in from the store. Send Beatrice for what you need. Whatever you do, don't touch any of the food or drink at the office, you hear me? I'll explain later."

"I understand. Now will you kindly get off the phone so I can make the necessary calls?" Her tone was salty, and I loved her for it. I hoped I was just like Frances when I grew up!

"Thank you. Oh, and Frances?"

"Now what is it?" she grumbled.

"I love you, even though you're a grumpy old nag."

There was a momentary pause. "I love you, too. Good-bye!"

I hugged my mother. "We might have a chance, Mom. We just might have a chance. Patsy may have already gotten through to Jeff so he might be on his way. I hope he understands my message."

"I didn't." Melody gave me a concerned look. "Are you sure you're okay?"

I smiled. Now my mother was questioning my mental status. "I'm fine, Mom. You weren't intended to understand," I laughed quietly. "Now then, we're going to have to go camping. Watch me carefully. I'm going to put your phone under this bush. Pay attention. It's the one directly opposite the gate to the tennis court. If they trace it, they will only find the phone, and not us. But, we may need to get back to it so we can't destroy it. I'm going to wipe out the calls—everything. I have to reset it to factory, so you'll lose your contacts and photos. Is that okay?"

"I don't have any friends up here and I sure haven't been taking pictures, dear, so reset away." My mother was such an innocent to have lived in so much hell her entire life.

I thank God that Melody had chosen that particular night to be lucid. I reset the phone, knowing they could still retrieve information with the right equipment, but it would stall them for the time being.

I went behind one of the cottages and told her, "Now, stand here and don't move. I'll be right back."

I sneaked around to the front of what was a vacant cottage. It was the off season, and nearly half of them were empty. We couldn't hide in one, but that didn't stop me from getting inside and stealing some bedding and the basket of complimentary snacks and drinks from the bar fridge. I wrapped these inside the blankets and scooted around to the back where Melody waited.

"Here we go," I said and we walked down the road for a ways to make it look like we'd started down the mountain. Fifty yards or so down, I pulled her into the woods and we headed straight toward the moon. It was the only point of reckoning available.

When I thought we'd gone far enough, I found a cluster of pines and lifted the boughs enough to scoot beneath them. There Melody and I spread the bedding I'd brought and sat down, pulling the heavier comforters over our shoulders.

"Are you hungry?" I asked.

"No. I just finished dinner when you showed up."

"Good. Me, either. We need to ration our food and drink. I don't know how long it will be until help comes. If it does at all. Now lean against me and let's see if we can take turns on the watch. You sleep first and I'll keep an eye on things."

She nodded. The years of living with my father and then hiding from him for many more had made her strong and a good fugitive. She didn't complain. She closed her eyes and soon I heard her even breathing.

Beautiful by day, the West Virginia mountains were a busy and frightening world at night. I heard animals moving about through the leaves and prayed none of them were hungry. In the distance there were owls and I'm sure I heard the snarl of a mountain lion. I wished I knew my animal kingdom a bit better. I could heal them, but hiding from them was something else entirely.

The night wore on and it grew more damp where we were sitting. I had no choice; there was nothing to keep us dry and Melody was sound asleep against my shoulder. I spent my time recalling in detail the monitors in that room. I needed to be as accurate as possible when I finally talked to Jeff.

DELUSION PROOF

I don't suppose it occurred to me until that
very moment that Jeff may not have gotten my
message. He might not have been where planned.
Something could have happened to change his
schedule, or unthinkably, to harm him. The whole
world would change because he couldn't be
reached.

There was no one else I trusted. At least no
one in a position to translate my message and
respond effectively. I told myself I would give it
until noon the next day and if there was no
response by then, I'd sneak back and grab the
phone and try someone at random at Walter Reed;
one of the senior doctors, perhaps.

The sun rose and I had to admit it was
magnificent. Melody stirred and indicated she
needed to take a bathroom break. "Mom, you'll
need to walk about twenty yards away and push
dirt over it with your shoe. Animals will follow that
scent and so far, we've been unbothered under this
bough."

She nodded and followed instructions. I held
my breath; afraid she'd topple over as she tried to
squat. I needed to take a turn myself, but decided
to wait until she was safely back.

She sat down next to me again. "Okay, my
turn," I said as I stiffly rose to my feet and went in
the opposite direction. Lifting my clothing, I had
just squatted when I heard a sound that made my

blood run cold. Without moving, I slowly looked to one side and saw the source; a coiled rattlesnake.

Everything I'd learned in biology escaped me in that moment's realization. There I was, everything God had given me bared and vulnerable and this infernal reptile was upset and poised to strike. Although this certainly was not Eden, the world's fate rested on the whim of a serpent. As for my bodily needs, that was a thought long gone. I couldn't have wet a leaf if my life depended on it—and indeed, perhaps it did. The creature lifted its head, the forked tongue shooting out rapidly as it debated its situation. It began to come closer, slowly winding toward my bared bottom. I stifled a scream and was afraid to try to run, knowing it was faster moving toward me than I could possibly be, rolling and then running away from it.

There was a loud thud about fifteen feet from me. The rattler was spooked by it and slithered away in the opposite direction. I looked up and there stood Melody, a triumphant smile on her face. "I've had lots of practice dealing with snakes," she grinned. I knew it was the human version to which she referred. I smiled at her. My mother was still tough. She may look frail and delicate, but she was tough through and through.

Emergency over, I took care of business and we settled back beneath our tree, rationing each other's drink and splitting a snack package of Fig Newton's between us. I'd never cared for the cookie, but preferences were a luxury we couldn't afford. It was only a matter of time before men from the bunker would be combing the mountainside and the road winding downward to look for us. They may or may not have dogs, but they would certainly have guns. I remembered the stables and realized they may even come on horseback, able to cover more miles in a shorter amount of time and with less effort.

I was so sleepy, but my heart was racing too fast to sleep. Melody understood and pointed to her bony shoulder with a gesture that I should lay my head there. "Just close your eyes," she whispered. "I'll take watch."

I did as she asked and gradually relaxed enough to fall asleep. She finally moved and my head jerked upward, re-acclimating myself to where I was. The sun was high overhead—nearly noon, by my guess.

"Have you seen or heard anything?" I asked, but she shook her head.

"Only you, snoring," she teased softly, and I pushed at her arm in a loving gesture.

At that moment, my ears picked up a new sound. Melody's face was unchanged and I realized my hearing was better. "Get back flat against the tree and try to block anything that's white or color. We have to blend in with the tree until we know." By then she heard it, too. It was the *thwop, thwop, thwop* of a helicopter. I prayed it was our side as they were coming from the north and not the direction of the hotel. As soon as one cleared the trees overhead, I cheered. It was, indeed, ours.

"Stay here. Don't move, no matter what. I will be back for you, I promise. I'm going to flag one down and get help."

She nodded and I pushed aside the tree bough and raced up the hill toward the roadway. The first helo had already passed, headed in the direction of the hotel. I heard a second and jumped into the roadway, waving my arms wildly. It pulled up, hovered a moment and then circled around and slowly lowered to the ground about twenty-five yards from me. A man jumped out and was running toward me.

It was Jeff!

My heart soared. Maybe we'd live.

Chapter 27

Jeff ran to me, lifting me up off my feet and hugging me. "I was so afraid," he shouted over the helo's noise.

I shook my head. "No time for that," I shouted. "I know what's going on and it's not good."

Jeff pulled me toward the helo and put me inside, pushing a pair of headphones over my ears. He tapped some buttons and suddenly we were on a conference call. The Pentagon briefly introduced themselves and then there was Jeff... and me.

"Dr. Amon," a voice without a name spoke into my ear. "What do you have for us?"

"Forgive the lack of titles, sir, but we don't have time. I was kidnapped and held in quarters that appeared government issue. Without a long story, I realized I was in the bunker built in the 50s below the Greenbriar. I was being held by Middle-easterners and by Dr. Milliken from Walter Reed; their resident psychiatrist. He's gone over to the enemy, sir."

"Damn!" I heard someone swear.

"I managed to subdue my attendant, a woman, and took a very short tour of the facility. I got into the control room. Except for the doctor, they are all Middle-Easterners, sir."

"Can you give us any idea what they're planning?" another voice asked.

"Sir, this isn't my field, but I watched the monitors and I read Farsi. I believe, sir, they are planning to drop biologicals along the East coast. Their maps indicate wind patterns and each drop designation has a fall-out area radiating around it. Sir, I believe they may try to use drones. The Greenbriar has an air strip, sir, but then you already know that." My voice trailed off in embarrassment.

"How many at the hotel? Any idea how many hostiles?"

"A rough guess may be a hundred, sir. Sir, there is a 60's version of a medical treatment area in the bunker. I offer my services if necessary."

"Are you injured, Doctor?"

"No, sir. I have my mother with me. She's hiding not far from here under the limbs of a pine tree where we spent the night. I have not witnessed or heard anything from the bunker since I left."

"Very well. Unless you have something to add, we'll take it from here."

"Sir, as a matter of fact, I do. I've been assigned an Agent over the past months whose name is Ester. I have reason to believe she is my half-sister, daughter of the Emir Faisal Muhammed. I believe I was brought here to witness the annihilation of the East Coast. I have not seen or heard talk of my father, but... well, sirs, if there's a daughter, there's also the possibility that there's a son."

"My God!" a voice burst out.

"Thank you, Dr. Amon. Agent Hansen, get Dr. Amon's mother and return with them both back here. We need to plan a contingency."

"Yes, sir," Jeff responded, his voice stiff. He looked at me as another helo flew overhead. "Where's Melody."

I began to run. "Come on, I'll show you."

We found her just as I'd left her. Jeff picked her up and brought her to the helo where we all climbed aboard. It lifted upward, circled a one-eighty and within moments we were high over the mountain range and headed back to D.C. I'd never been so happy in my life.

"Jeff, I think Ester tried to kill me using arsenic. I don't know why I didn't recognize the symptoms; maybe because I was so sick. It was so classic. I should have picked up on it. She had access just before I got sick each time."

He nodded, tapping his headphone. "Yes, we figured it out. Frances caught on and Agent Smith, Patsy, drew the same conclusion and filled me in. We're having the facilities and homes swept and tested. You'll be staying in a hotel until we've cleared the necessaries."

I nodded and leaned my head back against the seat. I was so tired. I wanted to close my eyes. I looked over at my mother. She was like a child, leaning forward, her nose pressed against the window as the helo wound left to right through the ridge tops. She may have the grace and behavior of a child, but in truth, Melody was as tough as nails. She was strong and capable. She laughed and clapped her hands. I looked at Jeff and blew him a kiss and then I promptly fell asleep.

Chapter 28

Once we arrived back in D.C., I was taken to the Pentagon and into a meeting room. I was surrounded by uniforms. I told them everything I knew, everything I suspected, and everything I feared. They were galvanized into action and I began to pray that they'd get there in time.

I learned later that all air traffic from Maine to Florida and as far west as Cincinnati was grounded so anything that moved on that radar would be considered an attack drone. The nation went on a full-scale alert and residents were told to stay in their homes, preferably in a basement and keep the doors and windows closed. I went over, in detail, every destination point I'd seen on their plans and roughly sketched the diameters around each point. I remembered there were six drones marked armed and ready and, at that point, none had yet been launched. In our favor was a strong north-easterly wind which would make it extremely difficult to pilot anything flying over the land.

A coordinated force surrounded and entered the bunker and, caught unaware, the occupants were taken into custody and flown to a base for interrogation. Each of the drones had been accounted for, housed in a nearby hanger buried in the woods south of the hotel. Lives saved were calculated in the millions. I breathed a sigh of relief.

"You're quite the hero, Sonia," Jeff told me, hugging me with pride. "There's talk of a medal and a meeting with the President."

"Oh, no, don't let them do that. That's just publicity I don't need. Jeff, did they find him? Is he alive?" I wanted no publicity. None whatsoever.

Jeff shook his head. "He wasn't in the bunker, but we don't know if that means he's dead, or just hiding somewhere else. It's entirely possible Faisal was in the United States. Unfortunately, we didn't see Ester either. My guess is that if he was in the US when the time for the attack arrived, he would have been brought there for safekeeping and to orchestrate the attack from their command center. I have no idea how you got in there and out again, but if you're looking for a job, the Agency will snap you right up – on a full-time basis!" Jeff winked at me.

I shook my head. "No, thank you. I've had enough of the Agency, thank you. I'll be available from time-to-time, like always but now I'd like a rocking chair, a cup of good tea and a sappy romance book, if you don't mind."

"How about a wedding?"

"That, too," I grinned and kissed him on the cheek. "For now, can we go to the hotel so Melody and I can rest and get a decent meal?"

"Of course!"

Chapter 29

Melody and I practically fell out of the vehicle after being chauffeured to the Hilton. Agents accompanied us inside as we were shown to adjoining rooms. I kissed my mother goodnight and couldn't wait to get into a hot, soaking tub.

Luckily, the Hilton offered complimentary bubble bath. I emptied the entire bottle into the steaming water, stripped right there on the bathroom floor and stepped in.

"Ahh..." I groaned aloud. I remembered the snake that had almost taken a bite of my bare butt and grinned at the memory of my mother with the club. I had to admit, though, the night on the forest floor after being held captive and fighting had taken a toll on me. I looked downward and saw plenty of bruises and scrapes. My broken leg had healed well, thank God, or it would have been an entirely different story. I marveled at the number of things that had to work out perfectly for us to be able to contain and put down the terror attack of that magnitude. If just one of the breaks hadn't happened, I might not be alive at that moment to enjoy the steaming water.

"You think you are so smart," said a harsh voice behind me. I whirled to see none other than Ester standing just inside the bathroom door. In her hand was a gun.

"How did you get in here?" My voice was frosty. I tried to control my fear.

"You see what I mean. Stupid. You are so stupid. I'm one of your guards, silly woman."

How could that happen? Something was very wrong. How had she gotten in here? Had they again infiltrated the Agency?

I leaned back and although my heart was racing, I said calmly, "I know who you are, you know."

"What do you know? You stupid woman." Ester's face was a twisted snarl, her eyes angry slits in her head. Her voice was shrill. "You should have died long ago. Don't worry. Your death is coming. Maybe as soon as tonight. Maybe in a couple of minutes."

I noticed her accent was stronger. Had she used this voice the day I met her, I would have known her to be Syrian, and a traitor to the Agency. "I know that we share blood."

She spat on the floor. "You are a bastard, born of a whore. Your blood is like the poison you consumed. It will kill you; I will see to it."

"And your blood? What makes it so pure?" My eyes taunted her. She was so angry I needed to use it to my advantage.

"My mother is not an American whore, but a beautiful Syrian woman, descended from royalty as he deserved."

I took a chance. "And your brother?"

She stomped on the spit. "He is the devil's spawn. I will remove him next. I am my father's daughter. I will inherit his power."

My heart had stopped. Just as I thought. There *was* a son and she hated him so he must have power, already.

"Perhaps I could help you with that. I'm a doctor, you know. Most likely he would like to see me, the first-born, dead."

"I do not need you to kill him. I will do it in my own way so there will be no trace. I will make him die slowly and suffer greatly." Ester's eyes glittered with hate. Her mouth was twisted and distorted. Her entire face seemed misshapen from anger and greed.

As she spoke, my eyes combed the room. I looked for a weapon, any kind of weapon I could use. To defend myself against a bullet? Was I insane?

"Since you plan to kill me, give me some answers so I will know how powerful you are. Our father. He lives?"

"He will live forever." Ester's voice was harsh. "You're an idiot if you think he'll ever die."

That didn't tell me anything. Was she just speaking rhetorically, as though he was a God or spirit?

"Yes, of course he will. He is a powerful man, Ester. Do you think you can take over his legacy?"

I heard the gun click. "That was the first chamber," she purred. Another stupid question and the second may not be empty."

Were we playing Russian roulette? It seemed so.

"Are there others? Besides you and our brother? Other's that will fight over Faisal's power?"

Click! I choked on my breath. She was totally mad! I didn't dare to ask anything more. My odds of survival were dropping by the moment. She also knew Melody was next door. She would kill us both.

I struggled to keep the conversation moving. "You're a fine nurse, you know. If you are willing, I believe the Agency will negotiate with you. You could become an informer and let them kill our brother."

Click! I wasn't going to say another word.

"Get out of the water," she ordered.

Oh, God this is it, I thought. I could obey, or not. Both would have the same outcome. I rose to my feet, hot soap suds streaming down my shaking body. My dark hair had been quickly twisted into a bun at the nape of my neck. I reached up slowly now and pulled it loose. My hair cascaded over my shoulders, across my breasts. I knew it meant nothing, but somehow it made me feel less vulnerable.

"Turn toward me," she barked, and I heard the gun cock. I mentally whispered a quick prayer, waiting for the moment when I would either hear another click, or I would hear nothing more... ever.

Click!

Tears added to my already moist cheeks and I began to cry at the torture. I'd tried so hard to survive. I'd tried to protect Melody and now it was all for nothing. I would never marry, never have a child of my own and never know a day's peace without the threat of my father and his blood-kin hunting me like an animal.

There were only two more chambers. That gave me even odds; fifty-fifty.

"Close your eyes," she ordered. I suddenly felt tired. So, so tired. I didn't care anymore. I wanted to just get it over with. I wanted the pain and the torture to end.

"Just kill me," I said in an even, unemotional voice.

There was silence. I stood there, quivering with a chill and the knowledge that I was about to die. But there was nothing. I opened my eyes.

The doorway was empty. Ester was gone.

I collapsed, downward into the still hot water. I fell with such abandon that half the water sloshed over the side; and I didn't care. Somehow, through the grace of God, I was still alive. Alive to be tortured just a little longer.

Then, I remembered. I leapt from the tub and ran to the door that separated my room from

Melody's. "Mom! Mom! Open the door! I beat on it with my fists.

She opened it, puzzled and then amazed as she saw me standing there, completely naked, wet and crying. I threw my arms around her. "I thought she'd kill you!"

"Who? Sonia, you're overly tired, dear. There's no one here. Just the agent in the hall."

I pushed her aside and into my room. With a courage born of sheer concession, I opened the doorway to the hall. There was only one agent standing there and she looked at me with alarm.

"Ma'am? Is something wrong?" She stepped into the room and shut the door behind herself, locking it. "Where's your mother?"

"In my room. Where's the other agent. Where is Ester?"

"Ma'am? There's no one else here. Just me. I don't know any Ester."

Everything went black.

Chapter 30

A cluster of seagulls flew overhead, their screeching overly loud to my ears as they fought for the tidbit of the rest of my sandwich I'd thrown up to them.

"You really need to eat more."

"Jeff, please don't fuss over me, honey."

"Sorry," he apologized, sitting in the sand next to my beach chair. "It's just that I'm worried about you."

"I know, I know," I sighed. "You know what? I just realized that I have never, ever, in my entire life not had to follow orders."

He chuckled and threw a handful of sand at the foam of a wave trying to reach us.

"No, really, I'm serious. First there was my father. Then briefly Melody and then back to him. Finally back to Melody briefly, and then I went into the Army. Since I retired, I've been sick and at gunpoint—still following orders. I'm tired of it. No more orders."

Jeff sighed, tossing a piece of sea grass away idly. "You know if I could take it all away; all the memories, I would."

"I know, but could we compromise and just don't tell me what to do. At least for today?"

He smiled and leaned forward to kiss me on the cheek. "Whatever you say," he emphasized and

239

rolled his hand in a sign of obedience. I hated that gesture. It reminded me of my father and the people he ruled. If he was alive.

"She wouldn't tell me."

"Who wouldn't?"

"Ester. I asked if our father was still alive and she gave me some oblique response like 'he will live forever.' What does that mean?"

"Sweetheart, we've talked about this. Ester wasn't there. You were overtired and the PTSD was probably roaring through you. There was only one agent and it wasn't Ester. Even Melody said so."

I shook my head. "No. You're all wrong. She *was* there, holding a gun. One by one she clicked through the chambers. I was down to the last two when she disappeared."

Jeff said nothing. He knew not to argue. That's what the doctors told him. To let me work through my delusions on my own. To argue would only make me hold on all the harder.

Jeff had brought me to the Maryland shore. He'd rented one of the colorful row cottages at the edge of the water and we'd moved in a month earlier. They said it would be good for my nerves. I was bored to death. I'd cooked all the lasagna and drank all the Chardonnay I could stand. I needed more in my life.

"No."

"Beg pardon?" Jeff was puzzled.

"I said no."

"No, what?"

"I won't marry you." I made my bottom lip flat; a sign that I wouldn't change my mind. I'd been doing that since I was six.

"Sonia! Really? Why not?" His face was devastated.

"Because I need to be more than just a wife. They won't let me practice until I swear that Ester was a mirage; a figment of my overworked mind. I know she wasn't, and I won't give in just to make them happy."

Jeff shook his head. "Ugh! You make me crazy, you know that? You already said you'd marry me, so I'm holding you to it. I agreed to postpone it until things settled down, and I keep my promises. So...will...you."

"Don't you miss it?"

"Miss what?"

"You know. The adrenalin rush. The excitement. The travel. The white knight in shining armor stuff. I miss it—I really do. Surely, you must."

His head was shaking side to side. "No, not one bit. I've had my fill of outrunning bullets and bombs. I'd like to marry the woman I love, settle down in a little house—well, maybe a little bigger than one of these," he gestured to the colorful row of beach cottages. "Thought I might try my hand at gardening."

I shook my head and smiled. "You'd suck at it. You're not the green thumb type. You'd go mad waiting for the plants to grow; no patience."

He pursed his lips. "No, I suppose you're right. Racing then. I'll take up Formula One racing and we'll travel the circuit in Europe. I'll win trophies and you can wave filmy hankies at me from the reviewing stands."

I rolled my eyes. "Now *that* I would suck at. I'm not the filmy hanky type; or haven't you noticed? Give me a syringe, a good case of Montezuma's revenge and let me stab it to death. That makes me happy." My eyes gleamed at the thought.

Jeff shook his head. "You know that can't happen; not for a while, anyway, Sonia. You need to find your way back to the woman you were."

I held on to my patience. "She's gone. That Sonia is gone. Forever. And not because of my father or Ester. She just wore out, gave up and left. I'm what's left over and I'm bored." My voice was crystal clear. "I'm bored."

We sat companionably in silence for a while, watching the waves endlessly roll toward us.

"Tide's coming in," he commented eventually. "We should move or we'll get wet."

I gave a hiss for a laugh. "Isn't that what you're supposed to do when you sit on the beach at the ocean's edge? Get wet?"

"I suppose. But then the sand will stick and I'll have to go inside and try to prime that silly water tank again to get enough for a quick shower to wash it off." Jeff hated sand. I supposed it was too much time spent in the Middle-East. "Or," I continued, "you could just wade into the ocean and come out clean without priming anything."

"Not an option." Jeff was taciturn.

"That's why you want to marry me. You're hoping some of that smart will rub off on you!" I teased him with my eyes.

Jeff threw a handful of sand at me on that one. "I want to marry you because I love you, and because I'm tired of running and of chasing and of hating and of seeing blood on everything around me. I just want you and a nice clean white bed."

"Believe me, you'll grow bored of that."

"Perhaps." He paused. "I'd still like to try."

Silence came between us. Jeff lay back on his elbows as he looked up at the clouds. "Could be some weather coming in later," he commented, pointing at a bulky cloud that rose upward like a chimney.

"It really was her, Jeff. It was Ester. I know what you think, but I'm telling you she was there."

"I believe you." He sifted sand through his hand.

I shook my head. "No, you don't, but listen anyway. I didn't tell you, or anyone else this, but she confirmed it."

"Confirmed what?"

"There is a brother. I have a step-brother."

He sat bolt upright. "What? Why didn't you say something?"

"Because you've all been saying she doesn't exist, that she wasn't there and that this is all my imagination. Why would I tell you about him if you don't believe me?" I knew my voice accused him.

Jeff swallowed and his eyes narrowed as he looked at me. "She does exist, Sonia. I know that. But she wasn't at the bunker and she didn't follow you to the hotel that night. We've been all over that."

"*You* have been all over that. I'm telling you that yes, I was exhausted and yes, I hadn't eaten and yes, my body was bruised and scraped, and I wanted to go to bed. But she walked in, just as if it was the most normal thing to do. She fired those chambers and somewhere in the middle of that, I asked about a brother. That got a chamber emptied and there weren't many left, so I didn't ask any more."

"Let's say for a moment, that's true." Jeff gazed into my eyes.

"Yes, let's say."

"What would you want to do about it?" He arched his eyebrows and watched me carefully.

"Not what you might think."

"Then what?"

"I want to meet him. I want to see my step-brother."

"You're joking." Jeff pushed away my words with a sweep of his hand.

"I'm dead serious." My voice was solemn.

"Why would you possibly want to invite that kind of terror into your life? Isn't this good enough for you? This peace and security? The love I give you and you keep pushing away?" Jeff's face was sad. He seemed hurt. I didn't want that.

I opened my arms, palms up. "I'm not pushing you away. I'm asking you to hold on. I need to settle things. Once and for all. I can't live in terror, Jeff. I just... I just can't. Neither can Melody. It's killing her, if you haven't noticed."

"She seems to be dealing with it much better than you are," he muttered, anger in his voice.

My mouth formed an O. "That's not fair. You haven't walked in my shoes. You know your life and where you're going. I don't. At any moment, Ester, or even the brother, could pop out from behind one of those cottages and shoot me in the head!"

"Don't talk like that. That thinking is radical!"

"That thinking is positive! You can't protect me from it if she decides to do it."

"She isn't here." He shook his head and sighed deeply.

"Maybe, but you don't *know* that, Jeff. No one knows where she is. No one knows if the Emir is still alive and perhaps worst yet, no one knows I have a brother."

"You should have said something." His eyes locked with mine.

"We've been over that." I stared back at him. We were at a stand-off.

Silence reigned.

"Okay, okay, what will it take to get this out of your head, silly girl?" I could hear the frustration in his voice. I didn't blame him. I felt frustrated, too.

"I want to go to Syria. I want to talk to people who know for sure. If Faisal is alive, I want to talk to him. If I have a brother, I want to talk to him, too. I want to talk to everyone, even Ester, and tell them to leave me alone and I will leave them be. Then I want to come home and live my life. Marry you and live happily ever after."

Jeff shook his head. "You know that's not possible. Do you really think we'll all meet and dance a Happy Jig and that'll be the end of it? You're sounding like a child, Sonia. You know if you go, he won't let you come back home. He will kill you. And if he's not there to do it, then she will, or the mysterious brother. Either way, you'll never come home to marry me. You'll be dead.

"Then I'll be dead. I am already." My voice was flat. I was certain of this.

"You're not going to let this go, are you?"

"No, I'm not."

Jeff sat up, dusted the sand from his shirt and rolled to his feet. He held out a hand.

"We're leaving?"

"Yes, we are leaving. We're going back to the cottage and pack our clothes. Then we'll drive into town, have some dinner and find a preacher. We're getting married and after that, and only after that, will we discuss how to get you into Syria or at least how to prove to you once and for all that there is no Emir, no Ester and no brother."

I looked at him a few seconds. "I asked you not to give me orders."

"I lied," he popped back.

"You always do." I was resigned.

We argued like that the rest of the day and made love as husband and wife through the night. It was wonderful. It was complete. And yet... it wasn't enough. Would my life ever be serene or close to perfect?

Would my life ever be truly good? Or peaceful?

The End
To be continued...

Continue reading with the next book in this series, Fool Proof.

Fool Proof

Prologue

I plunge my fingers into the sand with sensual pleasure, withdrawing them slowly as I watch the grains slowly cascade downward. The sun is warm on my face, and for the first time in decades, I feel safe.

Safe... that elusive feeling so wonderful that you curl your toes; as you do while eating rich chocolate cake. What makes it so wonderful? Is it the contrast to the days that preceded it? Is it the idea that it's fleeting and therefore, must be cherished at the moment?

Tipping my head back to breathe in contentment, a cold shadow falls over my face. I open my eyes to see a vulture circling above me. Using my hand, I shade my eyes and see that another has joined it; both gliding on the warm air current as though conserving their strength for the kill that lies ahead. I look around me for the intended victim, but for as far as I can see, there is only white sand. That's when a shiver climbs down my spine, and suddenly the shadow is cold as it passes over me, contrasting to the white sand around me which is now growing hotter by the second. The sand is intolerable, scorching me. I can see my fingers are red and blistered—burned. I pull back in alarm, grabbing for the cover on which I lay, but it's no longer there. The vultures come lower. My protection is gone. No gun, no rocks, not even a syringe. I am utterly helpless and must wait. To run would mean burning my feet and they know this. They will ride the warm currents until I've been driven mad by the possibilities. Until I am dead. Then they will come. Then they will feast. Then I will know nothing ever again.

With an enormous sucking breath, I sat up in the bed. There was a movement to my left, and in my confusion, I cried out, a frightening, inarticulate sound in the darkness.

"Sonia, honey, it's me. Jeff. Did you have a bad dream?" Jeff touched my shoulder, a concerned look on his handsome face.

I nodded, but it was still too hot to cry. The tears would sizzle on my cheeks, and I'd be scarred. "I'm so hot. So very, very hot."

His hand moved to cover my forehead. "Nooo, you're fine. It was just a nightmare, sweetheart. You're here with me now, and perfectly safe."

I shook my head. "No, I'm burning up."

I felt him move, and then he was lifting me into the air, cradling me against his chest. I saw the glare of light off the white tile of our bathroom, and then he was standing me in the shower. A cooling rain flowed over me, and Jeff came in with me; both of us in our nightclothes. "That better?" he asked, his voice concerned.

"Ohhhh, yes, much better," I relent mentally. "Much, much, better." I offered him a grateful look.

"Silly girl, what would you do without me?"

"I'd die. I know that I would." My tone was serious. I truly believed that.

"Oh, God, no. You're the strongest woman I know." Jeff's hazel eyes bored into mine.

"Let's hope you're right, but I'm not so sure." There was at least one who was stronger. For me to live, she had to die."

Chapter 1

"Jeff, do you think uncertainties give us a better life?"

He handed me coffee in my favorite yellow mug and sat in the lounger next to me. Our patio was lovely that time of year. I had discovered the simple joys—a healing exercise—and hung bird feeders everywhere one looked. A trellis with clematis was in full bloom. Bees were shopping for their autumn feasts among the late summer blossoms of the hostas and daylilies. I often remarked it was the one place I'd found where life could truly be in balance. I was at peace on my patio. I felt safe.

"A better life?" Jeff arched his eyebrows. "Can't say that's something I've dwelled much on, sweetheart, but I suppose it forces us not to take things for granted. We never know and you, if anyone, should be an expert on that. Why do you ask?"

I pondered his question. "As a physician, I've been trained to go through mental checklists when diagnosing a patient. I suppose it's trained my perception of almost everything in life."

"It was that dream, wasn't it?" Jeff's voice was soft.

"They're never innocent, you know." My dark eyes were shadowed beneath from the lack of renewing sleep.

"I know they scare the crap out of you." He reached for my hand. I believe he did know how terrified I was.

"It's more than that. Those nightmares feed the uncertainties about my life in general. Sometimes I feel like someone is trying to communicate with me, there in my dreams. It's eerie."

"Have you considered sleeping pills?"

I shook my head impatiently and released a brief burst of exasperation. "You know I don't believe in that. At least not for me. No, I must deal with my demons head-on, or they won't leave me in peace. Not ever." My voice was defiant.

"Why do I feel like you're working up to an announcement?" Jeff shook his head as a shadow passed across his face.

I turned to smile at him, tipping my head slightly in a cajoling manner. "You know me so well, don't you?"

Jeff grinned and shook his head. "Here it comes. I should know you best. I've been in charge of you longer than anyone, and that includes Melody."

"Oh, let's leave her out of this." My mother was a beautiful, innocent spirit. "She's had enough woes and is finally feeling a little peaceful." I paused. "I will say I'm concerned. She's gotten confused the last few times I've spoken to her and it concerns me."

"Confused, as in an aging process?"

I shrugged my shoulders. "Can't say. She's been through so much her brain must seem like swiss cheese—addled at the very least. I'm sure she has gaping holes with memories she pushes away. She's not ill, just worn out with worrying is all – or at least that's what I think at this time."

"How about her daughter?"

I shook my head. "The Emir hasn't broken me yet, and neither will Ester. As for my possible brother, I've yet to know much about him. For all I know, he may be an addle-pated weakling."

Jeff gave a wry chuckle. "Not likely, with your father donating to his genetics."

"No," I sighed. "I think you're probably right." I smiled at him. "But, I can wish, can't I?"

Jeff sighed. "Okay, so out with it. Where is this long speech of introspection leading you to tell me?"

I set my coffee down and turned sideways on the lounger so I could look straight into his eyes. "I'm not telling, Jeff. I'm asking."

"Oh, really?" he laughed. "What if I refuse?"

"Hear me out, first. Then, if you want to refuse, I'll go alone."

"I knew it!" he declared. "It's that cock-eyed determination to go back to Syria, isn't it?" Jeff wasn't happy. We'd had this conversation several times.

I held on to my temper. Hadn't my mother always said you could catch more bees with honey? "Jeff, put yourself in my shoes. I can't rest until I know who is or is not controlling my life. I'm looking over my shoulder everywhere I go. Sometimes I convince myself that my father is dead, that the evil is gone for good. And then, without expecting it, Ester shows up, and I see her dark, evil face, and it puts the fear of God in me. I can't help that. I can't get better until I know that I'm safe." I truly hoped he understood. I was tired of trying to explain it to him.

"Sonia, do you seriously believe that you can go to Syria and find your answers without him or her finding you first? And what if there is a brother? What if the Emir is gone and the brother has taken over? You are his firstborn. For that reason alone, you are a threat to both, don't you see that?" Jeff held on to his patience.

"Of course, I do," I snapped. "But Jeff, it's like trying to navigate the Amazon jungle with the paper bag over my head. I don't know what's out there and I can't see to learn. It's unnerving. More than that, it's driving me crazy. I've used all the skills I learned in my medical training. I've consulted with specialists, and even though I didn't tell you, I even visited a fortune teller once."

"You did?" Jeff laughed. "My serious, sober, level-headed wife went to see a fortune-teller? What did she tell you?"

"Now, don't make fun of me. Don't you feel some of that? You must." My voice was emphatic. "You've been with the agency long enough and have assumed many enemies. He must've made enemies in that time, and someone is out there wanting to settle the score."

He looked down and the tone of his voice lowered. "I know very well what you're talking about, maybe not to the extent that you do, but it's there for me, too. If you think about it, it'll drive you crazy"

"Yes. It does drive me crazy. Constantly."

Jeff continued, "There are no certainties to answer your earlier question. If you're going to break life down into computational Las Vegas odds, you'll find you're much more likely to die of an injury in a car accident or a medical mistake at one of your very own hospitals. You know that, I don't have to tell you."

"I get that, but that doesn't mean that you shouldn't - or I shouldn't - try to minimize the threat whenever you have that opportunity."

"Not at the cost of your sanity. If you go over there and get yourself killed, who's going to grow old with me?" A sad shadow crossed his face. "Who's going to look after Melody? Who's going to heal the men who show up with battle wounds, and don't tell me you retired from that, I know better. I know that you go to the hospital and hang out when you feel useless and afraid."

I was surprised. "How did you know that? Frances told you, didn't she?" Frances, my secretary, must have snitched on me.

"Now, don't go blaming her. She has your welfare at heart, just like I do. In fact, it takes both of us to keep you safe." Jeff gave me his knowing look. In truth, he was probably right, but I'd never admit it.

"Frances oversteps sometimes," I grumbled.

"She may, but I'll bet she isn't visiting fortune-tellers."

I looked away from my husband. For a moment I wished I'd not told him about the fortune teller. I knew his methodical brain wouldn't be able to process it.

Would you like to read more of, Fool Proof, the continuing story of Sonia?

Thank you so much for reading *Delusion Proof,* the second book in the Dr. Sonia Amon Medical Thriller series. I hope you enjoyed it and that you'll become one of my regular readers. If you did enjoy this, please consider leaving me a review.

I love connecting with you so feel free to join my Readers Lounge on Facebook or my mailing list at www.judithlucci.com. I can also be reached at judithlucciwrites@gmail.com

Judith

Made in the USA
Monee, IL
21 April 2021